Editor	Robert Stapleton
Managing Editor	JD Amick
Associate Editor	Ashley Petry
Fiction Editor	Jeff Marvel
Poetry Editor	Bek Primrose
Nonfiction Editor	Katie Hilton
Web Manager	Bree Flannelly
Social Media	Kellie Stewart
Intern	Katie Peterson

Readers Aanuoluwapo Adesina, Eric Baugh, Rosemary Freedman, Amy Gastelum, Abby Goertzen, Meggyn Keeley, Susan Lerner, Allison Moran, Stephanie Perkins, Katie Peterson, Elizabeth Reames, Mac Scott, Kellie Stewart, John Strauss

Cover Art	"Night Ride" by Haylee Morice
Design & Layout	Kayla E./Design Altar

We publish new material on our website on the first Friday of every month, along with two print issues per year. We invite electronic submissions only from September 1 to March 31 at booth.submittable.com/submit. Full guidelines on website.

We are grateful for the ongoing support of the Butler University MFA program and the College of Liberal Arts & Sciences at Butler University.

ISSN 23332-4813
ISBN 978-0-9961641-0-8

A 1-year print subscription is $15. Send to:
Booth/Butler University
4600 Sunset Ave
Indianapolis, IN 46228

Visit us online:
booth.butler.edu

contents

FICTION

05 Hosting
Emily Lawson

71 Miss Texas Considers
Talking about Her Tooth
Corey Miller

77 Sunny
Allison Kade

115 You Are Enough
Timothy Day

149 The Currency of Secrets
Ruyi Wen

NONFICTION

49 Skateaway
Jillian Luft

93 Soul to Keep
Rochelle Hurt

127 Country of the Blind
Brittany Hailer

139 Duty
Jax Connelly

INTERVIEWS

24 A Conversation
with Eula Biss
Susan Lerner

102 A Conversation
with sam sax
Abby Johnson

POETRY

01 Elegy for the Four Chambers
of My Mother's Heart
Steven Espada Dawson

46 First Date with the Asteroid
that Killed the Dinosaurs
Katie McMorris

69 World Music and Arts
Festival, Santiago, Chile
David Brunson

74 Split Portrait
Jane Morton

91 Mom, when I called
Taylor Kirby

101 Sisters Sharing a Pillow, or,
"Thank You, 117 Lomia"
A. Prevett

113 under bridges
Emilie Collyer

124 Care
Ciona Rouse

134 Wedding Vows First Draft
Claire Denson

136 Splitting the Cracks
Claire Denson

152 I Star It Out
Erika Walsh

COMICS

63 Heaven Help Me
Eva Sterrett

ELEGY FOR THE FOUR CHAMBERS OF MY MOTHER'S HEART

Steven Espada Dawson

i.
You're just barely making it now
to the microwave. Your knees,

they tremble, Mom, like a fresh fawn.
The beginning of life is too much

like the end of it. You pinch the seam
of a bag of popcorn, swaddle it

like a steaming newborn within the basket
of your walker. Did you know, you ask,

that Orville Redenbacher died sleeping
in a jacuzzi? That's how I want to go.

ii.
As a child you made me hold my breath
driving past cemeteries, under bridges,
through tunnels. We gasped for air

like superstitious carp, tiptoed
around grave plots to honor the dead,
leaped over sidewalk cracks to honor
the living: our mothers, you. You ratchet

the bare ball of your foot into each seam
as if it were the cherry end of a cigarette.

As if you could design a future for yourself,
trade chemotherapy for a chiropractor.
On that last flight to see you, the pilot said

if you insist on smoking, please do it outside.
At the Olive Garden off Sable Boulevard,
you joke: when you're here, your family

is dying. We push yardsticks of bread down
our trombone throats, wonder how
to prolong a meal that must end.

iii.
In Colorado, you work nights
at a call center from your

kitchen table. You swore once
you sold camping gear

to Matthew McConaughey,
kept his credit card number

for a rainy day. The graveyard
shift should be illegal, I joke.
You throw your head
back in laughter, like a villain

might in a Disney movie—
Ursulaesque. You say dying

doesn't keep the lights on,
the water heater drooling

in its sarcophagus closet.
But you're off tonight.

You get to sleep in the dark,
like regular people, you say.

iv.
This is an elegy, and believe me it will end
within the small walls of your townhome.

And because I am selfish it ends with your
words and a memory of just you and me

standing above your kitchen sink, pouring
water into an ice cube tray. You tell me

to watch as the water fills up one corner,
then overflows into every empty square.

This, you say, this is how I love you.

HOSTING

Emily Lawson

DAY 1—

I have never been offered this much money to starve. Rather: to starve, then to eat again at last while the other woman plugs in. Marcia. I often wonder what she looks like. We have spoken on the phone. I picture her blond, standing over a farmhouse sink full of gardenias. But a woman who can afford this obscene treat does not do her own dishes or arrange her own flowers. She wears a cream-colored blouse of heavy matte silk; she crosses her ankles on a wicker deck chair. I cannot decide on her figure: I assume she is neither large nor small. Perhaps she likes movies like *Cast Away*, and watching is not enough. She wants to drag herself through the sand by her dirt-blackened, broken nails, sun scarred, blind with need, toward a grimy coconut that has washed ashore; to smash it over and over against a rock; to feel the last of her strength, cracking the hull, prying it open; and then to suck its divine fatty marrow, rocking with pleasure.

Some clients pay for that very package. They fly by private jet to an island, where they have planted some desperate host to scrabble and starve, trying to catch fish with their hands for a few weeks, building little fires. I have thought of trying it, but I mean this time to be my last.

I've read reviews—perhaps Marcia has too—of these adventures. The problem: the twenty minutes or so you can maintain the bond is not enough. You feel the host's hunger, yes, but it gets lost in all the other bodily shocks: the salt-cured sunburn, the dizziness, the chapped and infected lips—you have to want to suffer some. But most distracting (one client wrote) is the filth: the sudden awareness of clumped, greasy hair, a foul taste in the foreign mouth. And, worst of all, the overwhelming odor of your (another person's) dirty body. It ruins the immersion—it is too strange, I guess, to smell like someone else. Most would rather watch others suffer on television.

And so I will stay in my apartment, bathing, drinking water, and seeing no one.

DAY 2—

The first day is nothing. Cake. On the second day, an untouchable itch reaches everywhere and nowhere. My stomach growls and aches.

I read that some bodybuilders find it exhausting to eat all the food they need to keep growing. What whiners. Until yesterday, I would wake up and have two fried eggs on buttery toast, with a mess of potatoes and a milkshake. Why not? I felt my stomach stretch—I could eat more and more. With mild pride I watched my belly button deepen and my breasts swell. I lifted weights each day to build as much muscle as I could, and rode my bike in the sun, stopping, if I wished, for an ice cream. Day two, and my thoughts already linger on food. If I didn't like eating, I wouldn't be worth so much.

Nothing to eat here now, though I have fit the cabinets with empty cereal boxes, empty cans, empty wine bottles, which I have been saving for weeks. If Marcia ever sees the footage, I want her to think the temptation is real as I open and close the cabinets, open and close the cabinets. I am not sure why—she did not ask me to do this. Perhaps it is for my own comfort.

DAY 3—

I had planned to read a stack of classics but have not touched one yet. Why? What else is there to do? Watering my plants, scrolling on my phone, watching stupid shows, as usual. My hunger coils, expands, and clenches. It is early spring, and I open the windows in the afternoons to let air through the house. I feel like I am waiting for someone to come home in the evening. But I've been alone three years now—divorced, already, longer than married.

If I go outside, I will crack in two minutes. I want to run cussing from the house to the nearby Mexican restaurant. I want to order a plate of enchiladas sizzling in rich sauce, refried beans drizzled with white cheese, and a mound of glossy yellow rice. I remind myself I've done this all before—all I have to do is nothing.

Of course, the point is not for it to be easy: the point is to be overwhelmed with desire. This time, when I pass the point of wanting food, I will have to make myself want it again.

Hunger pangs have stopped, on schedule. My breath is so foul with ketosis, already, that I gargle every hour. My throat burns. My gut is churning and purging. I find all of this awful. But of course I have a talent for it. As a kid, I loved reality TV—*Fear Factor* and *Survivor*, *Naked and Afraid*. While my siblings shrieked and squirmed, I leaned in. I would have done it, I said, for the prize. The rewards were so staggering—I would think of all I could buy if I won, and I would. I pictured myself doing each dreadful thing: lying still in a clear vat full of maggots, swallowing each bite of a bull's barbecued penis without retching, being buried alive in a coffin while the little green light of the camera lit my face like a ghoul's.

Where did they get all those maggots?

Filled with manic energy this morning, then crashed. My family thinks I am at a silent meditation retreat in Colorado. They won't investigate. They think I have done several shorter retreats already, and that those weeks changed my life. I watch them online, scrolling through photos, remembering to leave no likes or little hearts. I am supposed to be sleeping on a hard mat and waking at dawn to the sound of a gong. Instead I wake in the rumpled mess of my deep bed at eleven, at noon. My sister has a picnic with my small nephews in the yard. Homemade popsicles with floating bits of fruit. An acquaintance shows off her new tattoo, peeling back the cellophane bandage. My cousin has been laid off, but thanks Jesus anyway.

I like to shuffle into the kitchen in my slippers to boil water in my kettle, pour it steaming into a mug. I have a metal pitcher of chilled water in the fridge, and a bowl of gleaming ice in the freezer. I keep refilling the ice trays, sometimes plucking out a cube to suck or crunch.

DAY 6—

Exhausted. Spent so long in the tub today, soaking with bubbles and oils. I see no need to be ascetic: there are still other joys. Body lotions, face masks. Scents of patchouli, lavender, cypress, sandalwood. I wanted to drink those bitter oils: to throw back each charming little vial like a shot. As the bubbles dissolved, I watched the space between my thinning thighs, fingered the emerging bones of my pelvis. I enjoyed soaping between my legs, between my toes, lathering the bar in my hands. I imagined nibbling a corner of the soap, like biting into a creamy coconut popsicle. I dozed off and woke up in cold water, shivering in the dark. I drained the tub and drew another steaming bath right away.

Now I am lying in my bathrobe. My finger pads are too shriveled. Going hungry feels easy so far. But I have so long to go. It is important to Marcia that this fast is the longest I've undertaken—twenty days—that I am pushing my limits, hungrier than ever, mad for food. It is also important to her that I come well-reviewed.

"Cassandra is clean, professional, and a joy to dine with. Her hunger is robust, but it is not obscene or obsessive. She eats at the proper pace. Cassandra's mouth feels clean and healthy and waters pleasantly, her taste buds are sensitive, and she chews with savor. Her palate, while naïve enough to thrill in new flavors, is sophisticated enough to be discerning. She has tidy manners and was not distracted by my presence. When we took our first bites together, I thought I would die of pleasure."

I wonder what Marcia is doing. Drinking mimosas at brunch, or doing calisthenics in a headband. I tried to look her up online but found nothing. She must look something like me: if you want to focus on one sensation when you bond with someone, you eliminate distractions, and slipping into a body too different from yours can be a shock.

I tried it with my ex once, and it wasn't romantic. I felt my center of gravity and my body temperature rise. I felt the sudden hair on my back itching. The soft thing alive between my legs disturbed me. And of course I saw my own distant body as he saw it, from his height. Felt his faint glint of want through his bored, empty recognition. I was so zoned out over there, under a net of sticky sensors, my legs fallen open.

"What should I do?" I/he asked the air, though I couldn't answer. The large hands waved limply. You can use a host only once—then you have to use someone else. We were high, and had no plan.

My movements are slowing. My hand reaching for a glass seems to drag through the air. I don't mind. And the edges of things are bright and gelid. Crystalline leaves churning outside, white spider moving in stop-motion over the counter.

What will this look like, if she ever does watch? Dragging myself from room to room, staring at one thing or another. Too dull to tolerate. I keep glancing up at the lens today.

DAY 8 —

Nausea in waves, coming whenever I watch TV or read too long. I wish I had not painted every wall in warm colors, meaning to stimulate the appetite. I loved choosing those paint chips: *wet terracotta, petaled rust, Tuscan tomato, sunflower farm, buttercream daisies.* Now I think: *McDonald's, ketchup, mustard, mayonnaise.*

I know all of Marcia's favorite foods. I know the first thing I will eat for her: crème brûlée. I have never had crème brûlée, which is one of the reasons she chose me. She will again get to taste it for the very first time.

It occurred to me today to put on music. Perhaps I would even sway my empty arms above my head. But when I started the first song, I felt as though strangers were banging on all my building's doors and windows. I turned off the song. I have grown too used to the quiet.

DAY 9—

Woke from half-sleep, hypnogogic dreamlets. Tiny cartoon slices of cake for a doll, with dollops of plastic whipped cream. Red light from a flashlight casting over undergrowth.

Have been lying in bed fourteen hours, unable to sleep, dozing a little. My mind is empty. I tried to masturbate out of boredom, but the effort of moving even one finger, of drawing up vigorous scenes in the mind, exhausts me. Of course, vicarious sex is popular now. You can try the things you never would. But if you're willing to share a room with two coupling strangers, I wonder what you dare not do.

When I was in my ex's body, he ate some chips from a bag, lay down on the couch, and unzipped his fly. I wanted to say *no thank you*, to stop, but of course I could not. I/he glanced over at my half-catatonic form slumped in my chair, and felt no guilt. I/he sucked my large tongue around in my/his mouth and clutched myself. I/he felt this tacky damp flesh compress under my/his fingers and jump to life. Little shoots. Strange. And yet it was banal—just what I would have expected. I was struck by the dullness of sensation, but also by the way it suffused the whole body, the air, in a way I thought it did only with women. I/he did not look over at me in the chair, was hardly aware of that other presence. I could feel his thoughts, but not make out their outlines. Perhaps that is a skill you can learn. They were not about me. I/he stared blankly down at what the hand was doing. Much harder and faster than I would have thought. I wanted to look away, to close my eyes, but could not.

After, he said he thought I would like it. Hadn't I always been curious? He asked me to do it when it was his turn. I never let him have a turn.

And now, somehow, like a pathetic animal, I am almost aroused. Perhaps if I touch it slowly for an hour or so, I will get a little shudder.

DAY 10 —

Woke up angry. I think *Fuck you, Marcia. If you want this so badly, just do it yourself.* But that's the thing—it isn't worth it.

When I first fasted, I was delighted at how my bulk fell away, how frail I became. A perk. I turned in the mirror, looking at the body of a preteen. Dizzy, I tried on my lingerie, took a few secret photos. Now I know better. My muscles will wither, and my organs will continue to shrink. By today, my liver must be suffering. My kidney function is impaired, my immune system compromised. At the end of these three weeks, I will have lost bone mass I can never recover. My resting metabolic rate will slow nearly to a trickle, and it will not readjust until I've put back the fat I've lost and more. My blood leptin levels will diminish, and I will not know when I am sated. I'll balloon out. But my muscles will take much longer to rebuild. People say that fasting detoxes your body, but I don't believe in toxins. Or don't care. Whatever toxins are supposed to be, I have never noticed them, and I would rather be full of toxins than shambling around with loose teeth, thinning hair, rotten breath, and the dreadful nauseous vertigo I feel today, blacking out my vision whenever I stand.

That I do not enjoy this will make it sweeter to eat at last. Anorexics are the worst candidates for this ordeal—they take too much satisfaction in fasting and none in food. They have artistry for hunger but none for eating. Seeing a table laid out for them, they fill with panic and dread, shame and fear.

DAY 11—

The tap water tastes different depending on the faucet and time of day. In the morning, the water from the bathroom sink is slightly sulfurous, eggy. I suck at it. The kitchen water is more metallic. My favorite is the hot water that falls into my open mouth when I slurp at the air in the shower—warm, robust, almost brothy.

To stay motivated, I dream of what I will do with the money. I will pay off the interest on my loans; I will buy a used car and save the rest. I have begun to spend some of my payment already, on credit, which is motivating. I'm invested, can't fail.

My head hurts nearly all the time, blaring red and orange. I can't look at a screen for long. Instead I paint my future life in detail. In my head, I move through a morning hour by hour. But when I try to imagine my breakfast, it turns to ash in my imaginary mouth. I am losing my cravings. I have a backup plan for this, but it will cost me.

DAY 12—

Spent hours flipping through a cookbook, walking through steps in my head. I dice onions, I simmer them in olive oil, I crush garlic with the flat of a knife. I give up, walk to the bathroom mirror, as I've been in the habit of doing. My empty eyes, sharp cheekbones. I am growing zits on my forehead. *Detoxing*, I'm sure.

If Marcia hasn't looked at the live-stream yet, she might begin to look now—now that I am truly starting to wither. Perhaps she likes to watch my pain. I've heard that some businessmen pay desperately poor women to take meth, just to watch them writhe and rage. Earlier I walked into the yellow kitchen where the camera sits in its ceiling corner, wearing only a bra and underwear, bending and stretching to show my ribs, the jutting bones of my pelvis above the loose waistband. Look what I have done for you.

Today I broke down and called a number I've been saving. I knew I would do this, deep down. The woman on the other end of the line knows about me, and will come to help me for cheap. She will come by in three days. I keep walking to the closet where I keep the machine, staring at it. My investment. It's four years old. Marcia will have her own, of course: state-of-the-art.

DAY 13—

I want her to like me: I want her to tip me perhaps two hundred dollars, because she is so grateful for what I have given her. I also want her to resent that I am a real person she has done this to, with an inner life. It would be better if I had hopes and dreams, plans and a family—I would seem so human then.

Is she married? Has she told her husband about me, what she has hired me for? Does she have children, and do they know? Or perhaps she and her husband will do it together: perhaps he has his own host. I picture a young man pacing his own bare apartment, picking up magazines, perhaps trying, like a fool, to do push-ups. Perhaps we will all meet in the same room.

Of course, her husband might choose to use a woman. There is something so matter-of-fact about a man eating a meal. It's different for us. No matter how daintily we eat, it is always in some way obscene, guilty, voluptuous, for us to chew and swallow.

DAY 14—

This is the longest I have gone without food, it occurs to me mildly. Going another week seems both unimaginable and inevitable. I am not supposed to be able to stand it. I need Marcia to feel my yearning pumping through me.

I am glad the camera can't reach this back room. This was never forbidden, but it can't be allowed. Still, I am not cheating. It takes ages to drag the machine out, to sit by the back door. Slowly I unfold my card table and set it up there, out of sight. I hope the camera I agreed to is the only one here. When I have done this, I am so dizzy I lie down all afternoon and all night, ignoring my need to urinate.

It seems I cannot sleep anymore. I only doze. Once I wished I could live my whole life without sleeping, and so extend it twice as long. I loved being alive, awake. Now each hour pains me with its glacial passing. I watch the dark ceiling. I should listen to something, a podcast, a quiet song. I can't do it. What I crave most is human touch.

DAY 15—

My host came by today, said hello, and sat at the table I had prepared for her, setting down her plastic bag. The aroma was overpowering, mouth-watering. Maybe that was all I needed. The smell of fish oil made me slightly ill. My host was a curvy woman. She understood the arrangement. I passed her the netted cap, and she fit it snugly over her scalp. She smiled and said, "Ready." Painfully, I laid myself flat on the floor. I shimmied my cap on. She reached down and hit "enter."

Then a jolt of vertigo, and I was looking down at myself lying there, and I was riveted, I admit. I used to wonder so much what I looked like—photos never seemed to get at the truth. Even videos were hard to trust. This, I thought, was the only way to truly see yourself as you were to others. Wealthy women like Marcia hire people to look at them like this when they try on pricey clothing.

But now I have seen how emaciated I am. It looked like another woman prone like a corpse on the carpet, pale as a cave fish. My hands looked oddly large on my wrists. I have never been pretty. Of course, my host had no real interest, and her gaze didn't linger for long.

She sat at the table and closed her eyes, darkening my world. I could feel the largeness of this feminine body, this heft, even of the stomach cavity and lungs. Her stomach was full. It flooded me with relief. It was as if an emergency siren, endlessly blaring these past two weeks, had been suddenly silenced. I felt the lovely plumpness of her cheeks from the inside. Even her eyelids felt heavier than mine. To be in her body was such a comfort—I felt warmed and held, comfortable and benevolent. I could taste on the back of her tongue something savory under something creamy and sweet. Thai iced tea, perhaps, and drunken noodles. Leaning over the table, she inhaled the smell of her leftovers.

It ended before I was ready. I wanted to go on as her forever, sitting and standing, full of peace and warmth, digesting a belly of warm food. When she pulled the net from the top of her head, I wanted to apologize, but didn't. She helped me up, and tears sprang to my eyes at her touch. I paid her in cash I had snuck from a stash in my bedroom for just this purpose. She raised her eyebrows at me, and I added a larger tip. She left. I felt—as I expected—just dreadful. I cried for the first time in months.

DAY 16—

Marcia called. My first thought was that she knew I had seen a host, that she was spying on me. I was so stiff with rage that I let the phone ring, then listened to her voicemail.

"Hi, Cassandra. This is Marcia. I'm sorry to bother you. I just wanted to check in and make sure you were doing all right. Remember, you can always stop. You're at the reins here." She paused. "I also wanted to let you know the car will come at three on Sunday, not two. OK—I'll see you then. Take care."

I held the phone. Surely she was watching me hold it. I sat down on the linoleum, feeling as though my blood were still suspended above me. I hit the call button, but she didn't pick up. I thought of waving up at the camera, but instead I dipped my head between my knees to rest.

I texted, "Sorry I missed your call! I am doing fine. I am *very* excited for Sunday."

DAY 17—

Now that I remember living without it, my hunger is back full force; it obsesses me. I feed it by thinking not of my favorite foods, but of Marcia's. I need to focus hard on the right things to train my urges. When I feel this is all too difficult, I remember the yogis who would hold one arm in the air for weeks, fighting through the pain, until the limb died and locked that way, and they could never put it down again. They would go on tour, gathering crowds and coins. Some paralyzed both arms. I am not so tough. Of course, they could not dress themselves—they needed attendants, or wives. I do not know if the arms could feel or not—perhaps they began to blacken and rot.

Looking down, my breasts seem shriveled. Slight nausea. But I return to the video I am watching: "How to Make Crème Brûlée at Home." I watch six bright yolks run under a pair of beaters, watch sugar crystals turn to liquid and crackle under a sharp blue flame.

DAY 18—

I sleep and bathe, hydrate myself and my houseplants. Which are thriving. I want to eat them. I want to suck the jelly out of a spear of agave, or crunch the leaves of my peace lily like lettuce. Instead I chew on ice. I fall half-asleep with an unread book on my chest.

After the initial bites of crème brûlée, there will be other morsels to taste: seared scallops, lemon risotto, smoked salmon with cream and capers, raspberry sorbet, and—oddly—circus peanuts. It must have been hard to find someone else who likes them. How many did she interview before me?

I know I will enjoy this food. I also know this is not the way to break a fast this long. I should be starting with broth or juice for the first two days, before having a piece of fruit, working up perhaps to a mashed potato. But I will eat and savor, bring my mind into my yearning mouth. Then, after Marcia unplugs, my stomach will ache and contract—perhaps I will vomit. Perhaps she has a little vomitorium all set up for me.

DAY 19—

I am making my slow preparations for tomorrow. My instructions are detailed: I am to wear my hair pulled back in a ponytail and dress myself in an outfit provided for me. It was delivered yesterday through my mail flap: flowing pants and a matching tunic. The ochre fabric is dense, rich, and silky. It has no tags. I am to wear a particular scent—hers, of course. I'm given a full-sized bottle. Perhaps I can water it down and sell what's left online.

My instinct is to try to look even frailer, maybe by shading the hollows of my cheeks with powder. I don't. As a kid, I always tried to act a little sicker than I was, in hopes of some vague reward—another day away from school, another cool washcloth on my forehead.

I prick my finger for a blood sample and put it back into the case I've been sent. I have two pills to take: one hundred milligrams of thiamine and five milligrams of folate, to help prevent refeeding syndrome. They will be the first solid things I have swallowed, and my mind keeps reaching toward them. I set them out on a tiny plate meant for an espresso cup and watch them. I hope I can keep them down.

I rotate through daydreams of going unpaid, being scolded or accused of fraudulence. I feel as if I am about to take an exam. I watch more cooking videos; I work my hunger up to a howling rage. Somewhere a ramekin of custard is being covered to cool overnight.

DAY 20—

I must have slept a little, because I woke early to a thunderstorm beating at the windows. The sky split white with lightning twice. There was relentless white noise, an empty sucking and roaring that must have been wind. I knew other windows were open, I knew that a pile of books and papers was soaking, but I could not get out of bed.

I spent the morning in the bath. I shampooed my scalp with slow, bony fingers and went through three disposable razors as I scraped three weeks of hair from my legs and underarms. I nicked my leg and the cut barely bled, unspooling a little brown curl in the water. The surface was gummy with soap scum and clumping hairs. But I can't stand in the shower now. I drained the water around me and pulled a towel down to where I sat.

I want to look nice for Marcia. I spritz her scent onto my wrists and neck. I daub blush onto my cheeks and apply mascara. There is something grotesque in this visage: hollow cheeks and sunken eyes, made up like this. A sugar skull.

When the call comes, I stand too quickly, and the world goes black, my head sears—but I shuffle to the door, undoing the chain lock with shaky fingers. The world outside is almost unbearably fresh, like old bandages have been torn off. A slim man waits there, greets me by name, and offers his arm. I take it. I want to lean on his shoulder, and do. When the car starts moving, my head lolls and I fall asleep at once. I am saving my strength.

We jerk to a stop at the end of a coiled driveway, at the base of a large, modern home. We make our way to a small door flanked by potted cypresses. We are entering through the back door, then, not the front.

This whole time, I realize now, I have been picturing a baroque room, perhaps hung with velvet curtains. An embroidered silk chaise lounge for Marcia to recline on, a tall window. I thought there would be a small, round table laid with a heavy tablecloth, candlesticks, and silver. A fine French restaurant with a single table. Instead this ground-floor room is minimal and modern. Every detail looks expensive, but it feels as if I have walked into an empty museum. The aesthetics of the monied class always disappoint me. I am offered a seat in a clear plastic chair. The machine gleams and hums behind me; I see the black leather armchair where Marcia will sit. The slim man climbs a staircase. My pulse is coming faster now, which dizzies me.

He returns with Marcia at last. She is a short woman, fit but slightly stocky, like I used to be. She has dark hair. She is wearing a tunic and trousers just like mine, with a matching manicure and fluffy shearling slippers. Marcia is no one you would ever notice. She is the kind of woman you might leave behind in the washroom by accident on your way out of a restaurant. She is one of those people who was meant to be middle-aged. I drag a smile across my face.

She regards me for a moment, her hand on the bannister, and I see her face is lit with longing. She is on the edge; she is bursting. Her eyes are shining as she offers a shaky smile. "It's so nice to meet you in person, Cassandra."

"Thank you for having me," I say.

"Thank you for coming. Can I get you anything to make you more comfortable?" She glances at the man.

"No, thank you," I say. "I'm ready now." I smile again. I am cold but hardly care. I can feel my stomach twitching. I can smell something excellent floating in.

Marcia sucks her lower lip as she sits in the armchair. She places on her head a diadem of soft plastic orbs. The newest version. The man arranges mine, disappears upstairs, and returns holding the ramekin on a simple porcelain plate. I want to seize it, smash it to the floor, and lick it up. I unfold a napkin and place it on my lap. The napkins are monogrammed. I have Marcia's, and I find this touching—though she is only trying to make herself feel at home. The man lowers the plate and tiny dessert spoon. I had always imagined a butler tying a bib around my neck for this part.

I look at Marcia, and she nods at me. She looks like a child, wide-eyed, tensed. The thin man clears his throat. I look down and close my eyes. Marcia wouldn't want me to watch her go limp. When I open them slowly, I can feel her with me. I have been waiting for this, my fabulous treat.

I look at the crème brûlée, the glassy amber surface marbled with bubbles and dark nebulas. I know what to do. But my eyes flick sideways, and I look at Marcia's body. I cannot stop myself. Her fingers clutch the arms of the chair— her head is thrown back and to the side, her mouth open, like someone frozen in coitus. Though it can't be, her body seems tense, about to spring. She looks so vulnerable like that, somehow lovely. I have looked too long now, too long, and I force my gaze back to the food. My mouth fills with water, and I swallow.

The little spoon is heavy. I tap its round edge against the glassy surface, once, twice, and it cracks. I lift my first bite, a shard of hard caramel perched on a large pearl of custard. I feel faint, urgent—*sugar*. My hand is shaking, and as I lift it, the spoon clatters against my teeth and topples in slow motion to the floor. I stare at it horrified—the gob of it wobbling there. The thin man's hand appears in seconds with another spoon, as if expecting this. I take it quickly, stab it into the custard again, and push it into my mouth.

An explosion, a cloudburst. It feels like silk, mousse—I was braced for a shock of sweetness, but the custard is balanced. Tangy and rich, heavy with fresh vanilla scraped by hand from the black pods, it is not too sweet. The dissolving grit of the sugar lacing through the pillowy mouthful, catching on my tongue, is too much. I moan. I look up to see the man bringing a tray of other small confections, exquisitely plated. How could I think of anything else? I see the circus peanuts—two of them—peeking their ugly orange heads out of an eggcup. No time to waste.

When it is over, when Marcia moves in her chair, my stomach is stretched so full it hurts, though I haven't had so much. Still, I want to stuff every last crumb into my mouth—want to eat and eat, then lick the plates. I place my hands in my lap. Marcia sighs, stretching. "That was wonderful," she says. "Wonderful." Her face is drowsy—bored now. She is bored. She thanks me, hands me a sealed envelope, wishes me well, and climbs the stairs. The man helps me up. Once I am out in the yard, I feel my bile begin to rise.

DAY 24—

"I had the pleasure of dining with Cassandra following her longest fast yet. Inside her, I felt a ravenous, aching hunger I could not have imagined. I now understand what so many impoverished people must endure. While painful, the experience as a whole was exquisite. Cassandra was so weak with desire that her hands shook, and she dropped the first spoon I provided her. Her pang of grief at having done so was quite endearing. Though she wasted a bit of our precious time together, and though she was a bit chilly, Cassandra's ecstasy once she began to eat was sublime, and those minutes of decadence were unlike anything I have ever experienced. I provided her with the highest-quality cuisine and was rewarded with a sensory adventure. This was a profound personal journey for me, and it was a pleasure to feed Cassandra. I recommend her to anyone hoping to try something new." ✧

A Conversation with

EULA BISS

by Susan Lerner

Eula Biss is the author of four books variously labeled as poetry, essay, and criticism. Her second book, *Notes from No Man's Land: American Essays*, won a National Book Critics Circle Award. The *New York Times Book Review* called her book *On Immunity* one of the ten best books of 2014. Her latest book, *Having and Being Had*, debuted in September. She is known for tackling controversial subject matter, and Parul Sehgal of the *New York Times* wrote that Biss excels at handling our twitchiest, most combustible metaphors. She has received a Guggenheim Fellowship, an NEA Literature Fellowship, a Howard Foundation Fellowship, a Rona Jaffe Foundation Writers' Award, and other prizes. She received her MFA from the University of Iowa. In April 2019, Biss sat down with *Booth* to discuss many topics, including racial appropriation, anti-vaxxing as a stance against capitalism, and the danger of white fantasies.

SUSAN LERNER: In an essay you published in the *Seneca Review,* "It Is What It Is," you wrote, "Naming something is a way of giving it permission to exist," which led me to ponder how the literary community has named your books. *The Balloonists* has been called prose poetry, essay, and memoir. *On Immunity* employs history, science, myth, metaphor, social commentary, and personal experience and perhaps defies classification. What are your feelings about naming when it comes to classifying your writing, and how do you feel about the labels others apply to it?

EULA BISS: One of the things that shows up in that essay is my mixed feelings. On the one hand I recognize there is some benefit to having a name for what you're doing that you recognize and that other people recognize. For years, when I was first starting out as a writer, I was in what felt like an unnamed space. *The Balloonists* got reviewed as fiction a couple of times. It also got reviewed as autobiography, which was not how it was intended. Its shelving designation is poetry, and there are certain conventions in poetry that are not the same as the conventions of autobiography. One of them is, in poetry there isn't the expectation that everything will be true. *The Balloonists* is autobiographical, but not everything in it is true. I was using the expectations of the genre of poetry, that one can move freely between life experienced and imagined situations. So that book is shelved in poetry. I intended it as poetry. But if it's read and understood as memoir/autobiography, then there's a little trouble in terms of genre expectations.

I experienced a sense of coming home when I found this term "lyric essay," which emerged in the late nineties, early aughts. I thought, this is what I've been doing all along, and now it has a name. It did seem more appropriate than prose poetry. The tradition of the prose poem is a distinct tradition, and what I'm doing falls outside of that. It felt relieving to know that there was a home for what I was doing and that other people were doing it. To me, that term was a way to put myself in contact with people who were doing what I was doing, who were interested in what I was doing, and who had similar sensibilities, maybe similar aesthetics. There seemed to be all this possibility in the term. But this category that felt so necessary and, in some ways, freeing to me is also confining in that it's being imagined in a certain restrictive way. I know this is particularly true for writers of color, who feel like the lyric essay has been published and curated as a very white space and a white genre. When that term emerged, the collections and anthologies were being curated in a particularly restrictive way that was not expansive, was not drawing on all the possibilities essays might manifest. That's a very long and messy way of answering your question.

SL: I love that. The memoirist Alexandra Fuller wrote a review of three new memoirs for the *New York Times* and titled her piece "The Examined Life May Be More Worth Living. Reading About It Is Another Matter." She used the terms "glorified journal" and "sleepy musings." She wrote that poorly conceived memoirs, like these, serve up material that is better dealt with in therapy, and that these books are not worthy of publication. Aminatta Forna also wrote about this in the *New York Review of Books*, saying that she begins her classes on memoir by telling the students, "This is not therapy. If you want therapy, go and see a therapist." What are your thoughts on this specific criticism about some memoirs, and do you think a writer's exploration of her emotional landscape can be valid literary material?

EB: Absolutely. I think anything can be valid literary material. This has been happening with memoir for many years. The idea is that if a memoir is bad, there's something wrong with the whole genre. We don't do that with fiction. When a novel is bad, we don't say, "The whole novel project is awful and it shouldn't be done." There's lots of bad poetry out there. Maybe the majority of poetry is bad poetry. But that's rarely used as an inroad for saying that poetry shouldn't be written, or that the entire project of poetry is flawed. I think we all understand that it's difficult to write a good poem, and not many people can do it. I think it's difficult to write a good memoir. There are going to be a lot of failed attempts, a lot of boring memoirs. For my part, I pick up a lot of fiction that I don't like, that I'm not interested in, that is boring and sleepy. But I would never write off the entire genre just because I don't like quite a bit of what I read in that genre.

In my practice, I'm always writing through my life, not about my life. I'm using my life to get at questions or problems that I want to discuss. My life is not actually the subject, it's my way in. It's the same thing that is done with a character in fiction. The book is not about that character; you're writing through the character to get at an idea or question. The same thing is done with information. When I write from information I'm also not writing about that information, I'm writing through it to get to other questions. I wrote a lot about vaccination in *On Immunity*. But in my mind, that book isn't about vaccination, it's about all the questions that vaccination raises, many of them ethical, moral questions. It's about, what do we owe to the people around us? What's our responsibility toward our children? How do you care for someone who can't care for themselves? Those questions transcend information. In the same way that book is not about the information it contains, good memoirs are usually not about the details in the life. Most of what's practiced in memoir now is what's called New Memoir. The New Memoir is the memoir that uses a person's life to talk about something. The Old Memoir—which we never call Old Memoir, just memoir—usually is written by a man who recalls the details of his life. In that manifestation of memoir, you don't need to have a project, or a question, or a problem. That kind of memoir is about its subject, and I tend to find them flatter.

SL: *Gulf Coast* published a transcript of a roundtable discussion you took part in about the futility of genre classification within nonfiction. In this discussion, both you and Maggie Nelson spoke about the word "meretricious." You said you came across this word, for the most part, in writing that referenced women's memoirs. I first came across that word in an interview Joyce Carol Oates gave to *Booth* a few years ago. When talking about personal writing, Oates said she was not a fan of confession, and that "to confess for other people, it is really morally questionable." We asked if she would still feel this way if the facts about other people impacted the writer's life, and she said, "It's not illuminating. It's sort of morbid and meretricious." I wonder how you consider confessional writing. Is there a line of privacy—for the writer and the people she writes about— beyond which you see the material becoming meretricious? And also, how do you see gender factoring into this issue?

EB: The stigma around life-writing and around memoir is loaded with sexism. And there's anxiety around gender hierarchy. It's not unusual to find a woman writer who primarily writes outside of memoir, for example in fiction, and is really attached to her position on the gender hierarchy as a woman who writes fiction, and therefore feels the need to disparage women who are writing in a feminized space such as confessional writing. My connection with what is called confessional is from the confessional poets. Sylvia Plath and Adrienne Rich are important poets to me— important thinkers and important twentieth-century feminists. Part of the insistence in their work and the insistence behind a lot of life-writing or personal writing is the insistence that women's lives matter. The everyday, the domestic, the feminine, can be, and should be, elevated in our internal hierarchy of importance. I really do believe in that. All my work is highly personal, and there are definitely political reasons behind that. For me, there's a feminist project. It's this idea that there's life, and then there's art. And they're at two ends of a spectrum. That if you're making art, you can't be writing about your life. Other binaries are woman/ man or art/science. It's interesting that things can change their gender when you change their binary. In the life/art binary, art is masculine. But in the art/science binary, art is feminine. This is one of the things that reveals that these gender designations have to do with power and hierarchy more than they have to do with what's really happening in the work or on the page.

SL: I was pondering women's writing. When I listen for writing about the many issues surrounding motherhood, I hear silence. What books have you found that thoughtfully address the concerns of motherhood?

EB: Just in the last five years there's been a whole bunch of books. Maggie Nelson's *Argonauts* was one. Rachel Cusk wrote about motherhood. Recently, the silence you've been aware of has been talked into a fair amount. Not that there isn't more work to do there. Women are talking into that and rallying themselves to treat it as a "serious subject." Getting back to the idea of what's valid and invalid, I feel very drawn to any space that has been excluded from conversation for any reason, either because it's not considered serious enough or it's too personal, too private. A lot of what I write into is often considered too controversial to be polite conversation. Writing into the space that's a little bit forbidden or not considered safe or appropriate—these taboos are, for me, productive and creative.

I'm going to answer this question in a long answer because it's so important to me. You've gotten to something that's a little thorn in my side—the sexism that hovers around memoir and life-writing. For research I was reading Angela Davis's book about the blues, which is called *Blues Legacies and Black Feminism*. She writes about how the blues have sometimes been misunderstood as not being political. This is because it's typical for blues lyrics to be highly personal—along the lines of "My man left me," "My man has done me wrong," or "I'm getting on a train and riding." These lyrics are often following a single person's experience, and Davis said that it's a grave misunderstanding to not recognize the blues as political. The politics is that someone is saying, "My experience matters." That is a political insistence. Especially if you're a Black woman. Davis wrote this book long before the Black Lives Matter movement, but she uses a sentence that says something like this, that the message behind these lyrics is that Black lives matter. We now have a movement that is using this phrase intentionally, but it's already embedded in the history of Black resistance in this country. Black feminism is very aware of the importance of insisting that all of what you're experiencing is validated. Not diminished. There is political power behind that.

SL: That's a fascinating parallel, between the literary and the genre of music coming from a marginalized people.

EB: I'm interested in the blues for that reason. There's great writing in the blues, too. I started looking into it because I was thinking, where is our literature of resistance? And the first thing I thought of was the blues.

SL: In an interview in *Bookforum* with Miranda Trimmier, you spoke about the trouble that comes with approaching medicine, specifically a public health initiative, with a consumerist, "What's in it for me?" mindset. I've been thinking about how the culture of medicine has changed over the past few decades. It seems to me that for reasons too complex to wrap my head around, medicine has repositioned itself as a consumer market. We shop for cheaper prescriptions, for physicians who charge less for office visits or procedures. What ideas did you glean from your conversations with other mothers and with health professionals that might have given you optimism that one day we might see ourselves, especially when it comes to public health initiatives, less like individual consumers and more like part of a community where we feel responsible for one another?

EB: I remember crossing paths with a neighbor of mine. I knew from a previous conversation that she hadn't vaccinated her children, and when I ran into her again, she said, "I found out that one of our neighbors has a child who is being treated for cancer. I marched my kids right to the doctor and had them vaccinated." She confessed to me, "It just never occurred to me to think of my two little girls as dangerous to other people."

For someone who already has cancer, the last thing they need is chicken pox while their treatment is depressing their immune system. She recognized that. All it took was the knowledge that there was one child who was particularly vulnerable and whom she needed to protect. What a lot of people miss is that we've got vulnerable people among us everywhere. The whole public health strategy is about protecting vulnerable people. It's just that some of that vulnerability is invisible. There are HIV-positive children all over the place, and you are not necessarily aware of their status. There are children whose parents don't have access to medical care for various reasons. There's a realm of reasons why people might not be protected against disease, and this neighbor just happened to bump into one of them directly in her community. She had a real desire to do right by the people in her community. I see that all the time in the people I interact with, this desire to be good community members. That desire doesn't always translate into action, or into the action that would be the most productive. But the desire is there. And the desire is at cross purposes with consumerism, and with the consumerist mentality. For the desire to be effective, the consumerist mentality has to be shaken off a little bit, or disrupted, or abandoned in some way.

I just read a great piece by Barbara Ehrenreich. She's in her late seventies, and she's been through a round of cancer at least once, and she's in remission. But she was describing being really turned off by a consumer mentality around her own medical care. She was announcing that she was not going to do preventative medicine anymore. She's reached an age where she feels like she's not going to do all these screenings, all these tests. What prompted this is that she'd been given this screening for bone density. She'd been told there was something wrong with her, and it had a name. But then she was told that 100 percent of women at her age have this problem, so it's not a pathology, it's what happens to women as they age. She said, "You're telling me what I already know, that I'm an aging woman."

SL: The flip side is that there are expensive and potentially problematic medicines that can treat osteoporosis, but there's a whole other book in that.

EB: It is so interesting. But what she noticed is that her doctor had committed himself to a new model where he wasn't going to take patients who didn't have insurance. He was going to see only the wealthiest patients, and he was going to promise them all the tests they wanted. And she said, "I want nothing to do with it. It doesn't feel ethical, and I don't think it's going to better my experience as a human being. I don't think I'm going to live a more fruitful, happier late-life if I have every test that's available for me."

SL: Do you have a sense that there's still this autism question causing fear about vaccination?

EB: I think it's more diffuse than that. The autism question is still there. But it is other fears, some of them very diffuse, like "something could go wrong." Sometimes it's more specific; it's about toxicity in general. It doesn't help that one of our vaccines comes from a class of vaccines called toxoids. It's not because they're toxic that they're called toxoids. Tetanus is a toxoid vaccine. What that tetanus bacteria releases in your body is a nerve toxin. Just recently there was one of the first cases of tetanus in this country in a really long time. This boy was in the hospital for a very long time. He lived, but with incredible interventions. So I think one of the fears is of ambient toxicity that isn't entirely rational. Yes, our environment is toxic in various ways, but our exposure to toxins is so much greater from other sources than it is from vaccinations. That's the least of our worries.

SL: I recently read *Winners Take All* by Anand Giridharadas, and he writes about how the agendas of the super wealthy and their corporate concerns dictate what happens in our world, and that this pushes government to the back seat. We've seen this phenomenon play out in Big Pharma, with Purdue Pharma and the Sacklers' aggressive and misleading marketing of OxyContin that led to the opioid crisis. I used to practice as a pharmacist, and I remember my discomfort when drug companies sent representatives to me, hoping I would influence physicians to prescribe certain drugs. Now, as a citizen, I still have that sense of helplessness and maybe even paranoia about marketing drugs. All of this made me wonder if one reason mothers might withhold inoculations is that they discern a decline in the power of government along with a rise in the power of everything corporate. I wonder if, for these mothers, it feels like there is no longer any sector of the medical establishment that has the power to ensure that the best interests of their children come first. What are your thoughts about this?

EB: Absolutely. This is how I ended up writing about capitalism, actually. It was as a direct result of having written about vaccination. This is one of the ways capitalism is damaging our society. It's seeding a kind of paranoia that's not unjustified. A woman who was interviewing me on the radio was suggesting that it was totally irrational and unreasonable for people to fear the products of big pharmaceutical companies. I said, "You really can't say that. In the same breath that you end this conversation with me, you're going to cover the opioid crisis." We're all aware that big pharmaceutical companies are doing things that are unethical, and at the same time everyone is saying *but trust them when it comes to vaccines.* That doesn't feel rational, that we should trust them when it comes to protecting our infants, but when it comes to marketing drugs that they know to be addictive and dangerous, we'll be suspicious. Once you lose someone's trust, you lose it. In Europe, where there are other kinds of health care systems, governments produce vaccines, not large pharmaceutical companies. The state has control over vaccine production. We have a very poor regulatory system, so people feel highly suspicious of any product that's being sold or marketed. It is anxiety-provoking to think that you can't be really sure of anything—that the product you're having injected into your child's body is what you're told it is, and it's going to do what you're told it's going to do. Lies have been told about other substances. Vaccination is one example of the price we're paying for our economic system. We're essentially paying in children's lives for damaged trust in our economic system. For a great number of people in my circle who don't vaccinate, it's an anti-capitalist stance.

SL: I do have a question about fear, because it's such a major player in the vaccine debate. In *On Immunity* you wrote about fear being accepted, even among the best-educated people in this country, as a kind of intelligence. In an interview for Barnes and Noble with Mark Athitakis, he christened you the "lyrical epistemologist of dread."

EB: That's great.

SL: I know! I'm curious if you think we have, even compared to the time when you grew up, in the '80s and '90s, become a more fear-centered culture. I grew up in the '70s, which was the start, as I see it, of the fearful parenting culture. There were kidnappings, the Son of Sam, the Zodiac killer, all kinds of chaos. And now there are new social forces at work, like the super-billionaires guiding social policy. I'm curious to know how you feel about fear and how you see this shifting our culture over time.

EB: A number of people have looked at how fear around parenting has gone up. Just based on my casual interactions with people, I can see that parents are in a different psychological state than my parents were in. But we live in a time that is, by far, statistically safer for children than in your childhood or mine. There's a disconnect between people's emotional lives and what's statistically true. There will always be, here or there, a child kidnapped, but these stories are used as metaphors. They're used to say, "See, see, it isn't safe. Our world isn't safe." Over and over again that's the story parents tell each other: "It's not like it was when we were kids." There's that sensibility that I think does have something to do with capitalism where we feel there's no one protecting us. But it's also cultural. We live in a culture that nurtures fear. I don't believe fear was nurtured in that way for my mother the way that it is for me. And also enforced.

I had this big experience with my son. I do move slightly outside of the parenting culture, and I do give him more autonomy than most of the parents around me. I'm trying to make his childhood look a little more like my '70s childhood than these over-managed, over-protected childhoods. But it's hard when you're working within a culture, because cultures have a way of enforcing their own rules. My son loves independence and asks for it. He was asking, in first grade, to walk home from school alone. The school is a ten-minute walk from our house. I made a deal with him that I would walk behind him by a block, and that was acceptable to him. One of the first times my son did this, he turned the corner onto the block that our house is on and a police car pulled over. By the time I got around the corner, the policeman was talking to my son. My son pointed at me, but the policeman was mad by the time I got there. We were standing nearly on my front lawn, and the policeman was berserk. He was pointing his finger in my face, and he was telling me that this was neglect, and I should be ashamed of myself, and my child was much too young to be walking alone. It escalated to the point where I had to ask whether I was under arrest. My son was crying, and it was a whole terrible scene. The police officer drove away and that was it. But it rattled me, and it rattled my child. So the anxiety that people feel isn't just in our heads, it's being actively, culturally enforced. I went outside the norm for a little bit, and I had a threat of punishment: *We'll take your kid away from you if you aren't holding his hand.* I then looked up the law in Illinois. Would that be neglect? Could I actually be punished for letting him walk to school alone? In Illinois, until the age of fourteen, your child has to be under your direct supervision at all times. That just isn't going to be true up until the age of fourteen. You're not going to have your child under your direct supervision at all times. The message is that if something goes wrong, it's your fault. You can be held criminally negligent.

SL: I can't imagine how this impacts mothers of color. That culture of fear must be an even heavier burden.

EB: I still wonder what would have happened if I had been a teenage Black mother who came around that corner rather than a white mother who is a little bit older, very self-possessed, and very sure of herself in this conversation. When he said this was neglect, I said, "Not in the state of California where I used to cover neglect. I'm not sure of the laws here, but I'm pretty sure it's not."

SL: I want to ask you about appropriation. There are long-standing debates in the writing community about writing about race. One is whether writers who are not people of color should write stories about people of color. Some writers of color have taken the stand that narratives about people of color should not be written by white writers. They say that the writing may not be authentic, may not position people of color at the center of their own stories, and that by writing these stories the white writers are potentially taking away the opportunity for a writer of color to sell a similar book. Other writers insist that no matter the color of the writer's skin, they should be allowed to write whatever it is they want to write. I'm curious, because you're a writer with white skin who writes about race, about your thoughts on cultural appropriation as it pertains to literature.

EB: It's a complicated subject. As an artist, I will always be in favor of artists taking risks. Any time you take a risk as an artist, there's a potential for failure. The stakes are high if you're writing about the experience of somebody who is far outside your subject position. If you get it wrong, you do damage. I think the way to do it is to understand that the stakes are high and that it needs to be done with care and responsibility. I was talking with Roger Reeves, the poet. He came to speak to a class of mine, and the class was asking him this question. He's an African American poet, playwright, he does all kinds of things. He's in the middle of writing a work of prose from the point of view of a woman. And he talked about what he was doing to ensure that he did that responsibly, how he was having a number of women close to him talk to him about this character, read this character, and tell him how they felt about the character. Basically he was using his resources in the community to be responsible in the way he created this character, so that he didn't project all his feelings or beliefs about women onto this woman that he was making on the page. As a woman who has read a lot of literature by men, in which women characters are imagined by men, I know that sometimes they get it right and sometimes they don't.

This happens with race, too. There are ways to do it responsibly. I'll personalize this. Recently I did a reading at Sarah Lawrence from the piece that was in the *New York Times*, "White Debt." One of the students asked me why I felt that it was appropriate to write about Black women who had been killed by the police or had suffered police brutality when that wasn't my story. I'm a nonfiction writer who frequently writes about other people's experiences. I write from research all the time. If somebody is killed by the police in the country where I live, I believe that that is my story too. It might not be my story in the same way that it is a woman of color's story. In that piece I was writing about Sandra Bland in part to look at my own culpability and complicity. I don't think it's going to be productive for anyone if white writers like me don't engage with the stories of Black people in any way. If I couldn't or didn't write about Sandra Bland, then I wouldn't be able to think into how I might be dangerous to someone like Sandra Bland, which is what I was up to in that essay. The danger in this conversation is that white writers might avoid the subject matter, but it's necessary for us to have productive conversations around the racial divisions in our country.

SL: That brings to mind a movie I haven't seen but that won an Academy Award, *The Green Book*.

EB: I didn't see it either, but I read about it.

SL: There was a lot of racial debate about that movie. People were saying that the white people who spearheaded that movie shouldn't have been the ones to make that movie. Maybe people were saying what you just said, that if you are a person with a skin color different from the people you are writing that you should take that extra care, and they didn't feel that this care was taken.

EB: What I've heard—and I might be getting this wrong—is that one of the places where the filmmaker went wrong is that he asked permission of the family, and the family said no. If you ask, you have to be willing to hear the answer no and work with that.

SL: Are you saying it's better not to ask?

EB: No! Well, it's better not to ask if you don't plan to listen to the answer. Whenever I write about people, I show it to them and say, "Is it all right if I publish this?" But I show it with the knowledge that they might say no and I might not be able to publish it. If I plan to publish it anyway, there's no reason to go through that process. If you're going to ask, let it be a real question, not an "I want your stamp of approval." The other problem with that movie, which I have not seen, so I'm speculating into it, is it sounds like it's a bit of a white fantasy. A white fantasy of a kind of friendship that could have, and might have, but probably did not exist between these two men. In the end, that's what probably makes it a less effective piece of art than the art that could have been made from the actual relationship. Was it just transactional? Was it distant? Was it complicated by the racial difference? Or was it complicated by class difference? That would have been a more interesting story to tell, rather than telling the white fantasy of a deep friendship.

SL: Right. But then that might not have been the movie that sold the most tickets.

EB: Yes, that's Hollywood making money off of fantasies. White fantasies are dangerous. They do real harm. If I was a writer of fiction, I would really want to self-examine around the fantasies I was putting on the page, especially if they were racialized fantasies. What am I getting out of it? What are other people getting out of it? But that doesn't mean you shouldn't wade into the terrain. It just means it's tricky terrain, and you have to go into it with self-awareness and cultural awareness. And the knowledge that we're in a time period in which narratives are being treated like property, which I don't believe they are. What I mean by that is, there was a case recently about Amélie Wen Zhao, a Chinese writer who immigrated to the United States and wrote a young adult novel—

SL: She took that book off the market.

EB: Yes, I never read the work because it never made it to the market. The early galleys were read and critiqued. It was science fiction, and it imagined a world in which there's something that looks like slavery. A bunch of people took issue with her because she was "appropriating" the story of African American slavery. She was very surprised by this because she was basing the future world on a world she knew to exist, indentured labor in China, which is coming very close to slavery. That story illustrates the danger in treating narratives, storylines, as if they're the property of a particular group. Slavery might take a number of different forms in different societies and times, but they have some resemblance to each other. What the story illustrates for me is that we think slavery has been eradicated and it hasn't. Something that looks enough like it to be called appropriation is happening in China. This is why we need a more expansive dialogue around appropriation. A poet friend of mine, Robyn Schiff, points out that the word "property" is embedded in the word "appropriation." What we're really talking about when we're talking about appropriation is property. I do think it's dangerous, and I'm speaking of capitalism, to make private property out of things that have traditionally been communal resources. Narrative and storytelling have traditionally been communal resources that are not privatized. To me it looks like an encroachment of privatization into the creative space when we start talking about and treating things as if they were private property. That is not to say it's totally OK for white writers to go out there and write any old character they—

SL: But there's already a long history of that happening. It's such a concern. And a wound.

EB There is a real wound, but it's an inappropriate correction to say, "Let's just not ever try to imagine into anyone else's experience." That's a potential loss for everyone who participates in art-making. Not just white people. A collective loss.

SL: In the notes to "All Apologies" you wrote about your guilt over all the impossible apologies you owe your parents. In an interview in *Numéro Cinq* with Adam Segal, you said, "Becoming a mother has changed my understanding of impossible apologies." What do you mean by an impossible apology, and how has becoming a parent changed your understanding of these?

EB: What I was thinking about when I was writing about impossible apologies was all the foolish things I did, especially when I was a teenager. Foolish and in retrospect cruel things I did to my parents. Out of youth, and naivete, and a sense of wanting to break away—all the reasons a teenager might act out. And I didn't even act out as much as some teenagers do. I remember a couple of hard arguments with my father. I think the impossible apology is that I thought, *If only I could have just felt the gratitude that I feel now.* But growing up is coming into knowledge. That's what makes it impossible. I had to come into the knowledge before I felt the gratitude. I can still live out my relationship with my parents with gratitude and express gratitude to them, but I can't go back in time. That's impossible. The other thing I realized, as a parent, is that I would never want or ask for an apology from my child. I fully expect that he too will do things as a teenager that will be really distressing to me. I just hope they don't cost him his life. My stepfather is Chinese, and in Chinese culture family members don't apologize to each other because it's something formal you would do with a stranger. To apologize to a family member is treating them like a stranger, pushing them away. It's a way of distancing yourself. This is my rough understanding from what my stepfather has told me. You don't say please and thank you within families because those niceties are public niceties, and this is a private space and it plays by different rules. That makes sense to me now that I have a child. I think it's culturally important that we teach our children to say please and thank you, to apologize, but I don't feel like I need that gesture from my child, that I need him to apologize for being who he is . . . for not understanding something, or for being young.

SL: I didn't want to end the interview without saying how touched I was when I read that your son asked you if he'd be able to remember his life when he died, and you asked him what part of his life he wanted to remember. His answer was "loving you."

EB: So amazing, isn't it? He was about four when he said that. It is the most heartbreaking thing he's ever said to me.

SL: I know! I wanted to talk about this with you but felt it should take the form of a question, so I wonder if you have had any other heartbreakingly tender conversations with your son?

EB: Yeah, a handful. He has the capacity to occasionally be really profound and emotive. What really amazed me about that moment was, I thought so much about expressing my love for him, that it never occurred to me that his primary experience was the experience of loving me. I was so concerned with making sure he felt loved. What he enjoyed feeling was his love for another person, not the sense of being loved. That's what was so profound to me. ◇

FIRST DATE WITH THE ASTEROID THAT KILLED THE DINOSAURS

Katie McMorris

The theater seats won't fit his shape,
so we trade the movie for outdoor dining,

where I pour mint julep down his crevices.
So, uh, what do you do for fun?

Instead I ramble about Gaston Bachelard
and his obsession with houses, how I'm terrified

aquariums will shatter and the Great Whites
will come swallow me whole, how corn

belongs on pizza but pineapple doesn't.
What's home like for you?

I learn about his siblings shaped like
Scooby-Doo pasta, how he always dreamed

of leaving his orbit and becoming a lawyer,
the sun's chain-smoking problem.

Do you like being spontaneous?
I'm swept into space and he buckles me

in Orion's Belt, teaching me to trapeze
swing, weightless. When we're both tired

and my spacesuit feels crowded, I stumble
against his ridges, crawl into a dip and sleep

off the whiskey. Too long embracing him
and I smell like something I can't explain,

how I imagine melted pears smell.
Have you ever done something you regret?

He's silent, and I almost tell him how
Apatosaurus means "deceptive lizard,"

how my favorite movie is *Jurassic Park*,
how I dig for bones in every patch of sand.

Instead I smile and tell him Jupiter's
glow really brings out his eyes.

                We'll save that for the second date.
He carries me home, curled against

his surface like a nautilus shell,
propelling into Earth with a force that

shatters all the historic churches.
He kisses my forehead and turns

to leave, but I pull him close and we
spend the next hour snuggled like that,

counting fire trucks by their siren sounds.

SKATEAWAY

Jillian Luft

IT'S NOVEMBER IN FLORIDA. The sun is a pat of butter, pale and mild. A cool breeze ruffles the sparse slash pines and my wispy bangs. My seventh grade class is on a field trip in the Savannas Preserve, trudging through miles of wetlands, toting pads of paper flapping like heron wings. Our assignment is to jot down our reflections of this ecosystem—sketch what we observe, note how it makes us feel.

Squish. Squish. Swish.

I trail S. as he wanders through the marsh, all short-boy swagger and Umbro shorts. He is my height, four foot ten, but his limbs are tanned and taut from intramural soccer.

Squish. Squish. Swish.

When S. turns around to give one of his buddies shit, his hair is dark and shiny, rippling like the reeds. When he cracks a

perverted joke, his eyes are dark and shiny slivers of shadow—
the kind I chased across playgrounds on wobbly toddler feet. S.
makes me feel inside the skin, makes me feel body blood bones
bursting with ache. I capture these details, sketch them in thick
unwavering lines, never once holding my pencil.

S. and I both wear sleeveless flannel shirts with hoods. I tease
that we are twins, and he flings mud in my direction, speckling
my tight-rolled jeans. I recognize this as flirting and giddily kick
a glob of earth at his shins. And instead of fleeing, S. storms
toward me, arms outstretched, knees marching and raised to the
sky like he's about to score a goal. He is tickling and poking and
knocking me off-balance. Ass sinking into earth. He immediately
apologizes, pulls me toward him, toward the sky so that I'm
rooted again in the muck. *It's OK, it's really fine.* The steely fence
of my smile surges with electricity. For the rest of the trip, I wish
he'd push me again. That I'd fall senseless, at his whim, a solid
smack to the dirt while the world continues to spin.

As we leave the preserve, Michelle yanks me by the wrist.
She wants to know whether I like S. And then Kristen C. and
Kristin T. and Cristyn want to know too. I shrug like I've seen
ingenues do in the movies—a coy but giddy lift of the shoulders
to the rose of the cheeks, a cinematic surrender to the romantic
machinations already underway. When they giggle and collect
the escaped hairs from my ponytail, smoothing them into place,
I know that they believe I can play this part: a girl on the verge
of being wanted.

On the bus ride home, I pull the window down. The air
tiptoes across my skin, murmurs in my hair. My flannel hood
billows behind me as I catch S. smiling. I utter something sly to
make him laugh. He opens his mouth wide, shows me the gap
between his teeth—the cracked window I can slip inside.

While Grandma doles out more goulash, Dad ignores us all. He grabs the cordless phone, heads for the garage, slams the door behind him with a vacuum-seal whoosh. Before arriving at our grandparents' house, my brother and I are passed around like Tupperware to family friends and neighbors. While Mom endures yet another hospital stay, they take care of us. I can't remember the new ailment or injury that's led to her current visit—just that I call 911 and we're whisked away to warm homes where light lives.

We eat unfamiliar breakfast cereals around actual kitchen tables. Groggy moms remind us of last night's homework, pat their son's bedhead, comb their daughter's hair until it shines. We stumble on mundane family dramas with no sharp edges and walk away unharmed, mystified that not every home houses deep secrets about dying and divorce. One day I hear one of our temporary guardians on the phone with our elusive dad. I wait for clues to his whereabouts. When the guardian asks after Jerry and Elaine, I know he's living with our grandparents. This whole time he's been just a fifteen-minute drive from where he left us.

I hear this guardian consoling, her empathetic sighs: *You're a good man, Mike . . . You did the best you could in the situation . . . You lasted longer than most of us would . . . Caretaking for someone so sick isn't easy, Mike . . . and the drugs they prescribed . . . morphine . . . no, not easy at all.* What she fails to say is that he's also a good man who's fallen in love with his wife's former nurse, his wife's former friend, that staticky and impatient buzz currently on the other end of Grandma's phone.

I'm glad to see Dad again—even if he is distracted, even if he is a shifty-eyed ghost who drifts through rooms. When

I have him in my sights long enough, I see that he's changed. He's grown his hair out past his ears and wears a hoop earring. He's stopped smiling, laughing, speaking in TV catchphrases, speaking at all. He chews his nails to fill the silence until She calls.

Dad is our sullen chauffeur. He drives us to the mall, drops us off at the arcade, picks us up from rec center dances. He buys us music with explicit lyrics, lets us blast it on the boombox in the backseat because the car stereo's broken. He lets us drive with the windows down because the AC's a piece of shit. When he's not shuffling us from place to place, he shuts doors behind him, shuts us out.

It's in the booths of mom-and-pop restaurants tucked away in strip malls that our former dad emerges. He turns the plastic menu over in his hands, beaming as he reads each item and its description, seeking out the strangest and spiciest dish and encouraging us to do the same. He asks us boring but welcome questions about friends and school. He resurrects an *SNL* character impression or two. Even then, he is prone to wandering off. The conversation abruptly ends with his mouth biting the air and his eyes turning somewhere deep and inward. My brother and I then turn to our meals. We paint our mouths in the radioactive orange of wing sauce, poke at bobbing hunks of ox-tail, pierce mounds of sweet plantains atop paper-thin steaks.

It's the sound of our cutlery scraping against plates that jolts him awake and leads him back to us, his passion for food reawakened. He stuffs himself silly before helping himself to our leftovers. He licks everything clean. For a few brief hours, he is sated and without want. For a few brief hours, he is ours. But as we wait for the bill, his eyes begin to bulge with a different hunger and he checks and checks his watch until it's time. Time to head home and swallow the words dripping through the phone, those morsels of love devoured in secret.

✧

Michelle's my friend and I don't know why. She wears real bras, matte lipstick, pressed powder. We wear the same brand of jean shorts but they carve her ass into denim sculpture. During English class she once reassured me, her pearly nails on my downy thigh: *Don't worry. Once you grow boobs and get rid of those braces, boys will notice you, too.*

Michelle's flawless but she's no soothsayer. I catch S.'s eye before my teeth return to smooth, before my chest becomes rough terrain.

In marketing class, S. and I make it official. We send the signal that we're "going out." This means we hold hands underneath our desks while the rest of our class watches, our eyes glued to the movie that our oaf of a teacher crammed into the VCR before cramming himself into a corner for his midday nap. I can't focus on the plot because of the incessant chatter of my classmates, their immature hissings of disbelief, their nervous chuckling as they gawk at the newest couple. I'm afraid to face S. I'm afraid to do this wrong, so I keep my palm in his, slick but faithfully entwined. My neck aches from craning to face the raised television, my pits form puddles, my mouth goes dry. S. is nothing more than sweaty fingers. I can barely recall what I like about him, but I know that I do.

Michelle leans over, rests her dimpled chin on my shoulder, her chocolate curls grazing the milk of my cheek as she whispers in my ear. She asks me why I'm not wearing a bra underneath my bodysuit, why I didn't shave my legs if I knew I'd be wearing shorts, why I didn't take her advice and wear a darker lip shade. I keep my back to her. My mouth curves into a sad slit of remorse she can't see. My back hunches into an apology she can. Without explanation, I let go of S.'s hand and scoot my chair back until I'm nearly in Michelle's lap. She snatches dirty blond wisps from the front of my head, pulls them tight into tiny braids, reminds me of the rules: *Bras aren't optional, even for someone as flat as you. It's about the nipples showing through . . . It doesn't matter if you forgot your electric razor at your old house, borrow your dad's crusty razor if you have to, and remember to shave your underarms when you wear a tank top, sheesh . . . Your hair looks cuter when it's braided like this, front strands on each side, but no bumps when you pull it back, remember?*

I nod, inhale her words along with her bubblegum breath, and then get lost in my own.

Yes, remember. Remember you're not pretty yet but a boy holds your hand and you've dreamed of this. Remember you've dreamed of this to keep from crying, to keep from falling apart, from falling into the black because there is something you do know: Your body needs to be approved, wanted, it needs to make the cut. Because bodies that don't make the cut are ignored, abandoned by hands, by hearts, left in hospital rooms to rot and apologize for the ways they've failed.

Mr. C. turns out the light and plugs in his mini-planetarium. The walls of the custodian closet instantly freckle with the universe. He directs our eyes to the back of the door. *Who can see the Big Dipper? The North Star?* But S. and I turn away from the skies to crouch on the rough of the carpet, our tongues, tiny cyclones, swirling through one another's hard and slick spaces. Our first kiss. Our classmates form a circle, softly cheering while Mr. C. rambles on about belts, bears, and the afterglow of dying stars. When the lights turn on, I am burning and crystallized. When the lights turn on, I am infinite. When the lights turn on, S. exits swiftly and does not look at me for the rest of the day.

The remainder of our relationship consists of half-hour phone calls on weekends where we stammer our way through pretending to care about each other's hobbies, and a gift exchange on the last day of school before Winter Break. I give him a Beavis and Butt-Head necklace from Claire's. He gives me a beaded anklet—also from Claire's. At this point, S. wants to dump me but knows it's the holidays. He doesn't know about my sick mom or anything else.

I am still awake on Christmas Eve, nestled into the couch, my face pressed into the pillow when Dad gets home from the mall near midnight, muttering obscenities, running a hand through his hair while berating himself for the crap he's managed to scrounge up.

Shhh, you'll wake them up, Grandma whispers, pointing to the closed door down the hall.

My dad and brother sleep in Grandma's guest room, a White Musk-scented arrangement of mahogany furniture and ceramic music boxes. I take the couch because it's the room with the TV. It's also where Grandpa sits in his La-Z-Boy until dawn watching B-movies in silence, the ghostly light reflected in his glasses. I like to watch him watch his genre fare: bikini girls and masked murderers. His face, an inscrutable but placid mask. As his son breaks down in tears, Grandpa's TV continues to sell things at a loud and insistent volume even though it's much too late for anyone to purchase. The stores have all closed. Christmas is here. Christ is born.

It's OK, my boy, Grandpa placates in his gentle tone, putting a hand on his trembling shoulder. Dad tosses two small white jewelry boxes and two unwrapped CDs underneath Grandma's puny tree. The boxes contain sterling silver rings with crushed stones, one for me and one for my brother. Neither of us have ever worn rings. Next to the rings rest the new Color Me Badd album for me and Snoop Dogg's *Doggystyle* for my brother. The tree branches droop with the weight of gaudy mirrored ornaments. Partly rusted angels.

My brother and I spend the first few hours of Christmas morning silent and solemn, our throats hanging heavy with what remains unsaid. I cram my mouth with hunks of Andes Mints piled high in Grandma's candy dish, swallowing my stabs of disappointment with Dad's last-minute gifts. We brandish our jewel cases in the air with ringed fingers and muted joy. *Thanks, Dad. Just what we wanted.* But he's looking at his watch again, cordless phone cradled in his hands. For our red-eyed father, it's clear this year is the horror version of that classic Christmas movie, that we're his Ghosts of Christmas Past, reminding him of what he's missing. And he's afraid he'll never reach his Christmas Future. With Her.

After a breakfast of cookies and eggnog, we dawdle, gathering our hand-wrapped gifts to bring to Mom and anticipating our first Christmas in a hospital room. We've celebrated numerous birthdays among doctors and nurses, an Easter in ICU, but never Christmas. Dad's already idling in the driveway, gripping the steering wheel, sipping coffee from his ceramic mug. Sunglasses on, engine groaning. Grandma smacks her lips in disapproval. Hands on her pink polyester waist, tight perm shaking. *You kids hurry it up*, she grumbles. *You don't even know what your father is sacrificing for you.* I've never heard her speak like this. Grandma spoils us, indulges us, rushes to our defense with root beer floats and a kind word when any adult dares let us down. She is the first to defend us against Dad's *no it's a school night* or *that food is crap* with a *just let 'em stay up, Michael* and a *Cool Whip helps them grow.* But now it's a withering look and *don't you know your father has places to be.*

For the half-hour drive to the Vero Beach Rehabilitation Center, Dad is a caged chimp, gnawing at the dry nubs of skin cracking above his splintered nails. His boombox plays Michael Bolton CD singles, a Toni Braxton album. Songs about the kind of love that tortures the mind, the kind of love that is more than love and stronger than any word can describe.

Once our visit is over, Dad will rush through holiday traffic to drop us off at our grandparents' and turn right back around, hightailing it on the turnpike and driving the four hours to Palatka to be with Her. He'll have only dinnertime and the dwindling hours of evening to spend by her side. When dawn breaks, he'll have to return to us. But the trek—the strain and stress of it—will be worth it. Because She exists. I know this is how he feels because I know this feeling. It's the feeling I get when S. greets me in the morning with a gap-toothed grin, when he hugs me outside the bus loading zone at dismissal. It's the feeling of air filling the lungs. Of forgetting where you end and they begin. Of forgetting what's come before or what will come after.

There's no tree, no lights, no tinsel, no music at the rehab center. There's a holiday events calendar pinned to the lobby bulletin board and sad paper snowflakes lining the halls. There's both of my aunts and my other grandmother passing around gifts and a tin of Danish butter cookies. There's Mom anchored to her bed, surrounded by ribbons and bows. There's her wan smile when she sees my dad lingering outside the door. There's his awkward hello and his abrupt exit and his pacing the halls for the next few hours.

Mom jokes she's the youngest patient. I kiss her steroid-swollen cheeks and laugh. She rumples my brother's hair, caresses the back of my hand. The slow drip of her IV is meant to buoy her spirits—maintain her mood somewhere between jolly and serene. But in the middle of her self-deprecating quips, her warm professions of how much she misses us, she begins to doze. Presents remain unopened in her bruised arms, punctured wrists wrapped tight around whatever crummy gifts we brought.

My aunts cackle about something morbid from their childhood, distracting themselves from the ailing and unconscious centerpiece of these festivities. They distract us with a bounty of gift bags, some with tissue paper and some without. Some items still include tags, and almost everything is from TJ Maxx. There's the Miami Hurricanes Starter jacket, a double-sided Flintstones tee, the red Umbro sweatshirt I asked for that reminds me of something S. would wear. I want to tell Mom more about S., but it doesn't seem like the right time. Her eyes aren't open, and when they are, she's asking with that faraway look why Dad doesn't come in and join us. It's the look he gets when he's thinking about that woman, the woman my mom can't bring herself to remember.

In the Skatetown USA parking lot, Dad studies my bulldog jowls with concern and begs me to reconsider. I've spent the day at the orthodontist's office: eyes seared by fluorescents, ears disarmed by lite FM. Dr. Wilson manipulated my mouth with latex and cold metal. She plucked four of my teeth from the vulnerable hinge of my jaw. *You have a crowded mouth*, she declared before prying my cheeks wide. *We need to make space.*

Dad, I'm fine, I mumble, stuffing my cheeks with fresh gauze, metallic petals blooming between my remaining molars.

Dad acquiesces, hands me a five-dollar bill and says, *Just call me from the pay phone if you feel any pain. Otherwise, I'll be back at ten.*

How to explain that no pain will stop me from staying until the last all-skate of the evening. How to explain that I resemble a monster from Grandpa's late-night movies, but S. is here and I must follow him around until he will no longer have me because I don't have a bedroom, a father who looks me in the eye, or a mother who can tell me what to do to keep getting kissed.

Dad's hatchback rolls away, and I don't turn around to wave goodbye. Instead I stand just outside the rink entrance adjusting my floral Lycra top, clamping down on the cotton, mustering a close-lipped smile. The night hums with a muffled freestyle beat that swells into a bass-trembling frenzy when I open the door. A doll voice sings over Nintendo noises that when she hears music, it makes her dance. I catch a whiff of the timeless aroma of roller rinks everywhere: corn dogs and Marlboros with a hint of sock sweat.

Beyond the skate rental counter, the rink gleams like an icy pond under alien siege. It's like Mr. C's planetarium but brighter and bigger and way more immersive. Purple and green squiggles of light flash across the walls while a constellation of bright white spirals in the center. Silhouettes of preteens, parents, and little children whirl through the laser mist, the sound of their coasting wheels rumbling against the hardwood. Some float by with ease. Some totter and clamber and cling to the arms of those they love and hope love them— trailing like comets.

When I still lived at home, I used to skate all day on my back patio. Mom would begin to slur from the medications and Dad would slam his fists against hard surfaces and I'd slip through the sliding glass door, taking to the large slab of gray concrete with speed and bravado. Radio blaring, I'd glide in graceful circles, flying past the view of the backyard, all green and mysterious, beyond the mesh screen. I'd roll myself into oblivion, lost to time, belting out what my mom called "risqué" lyrics until dusk fell. Then I'd reluctantly plod into the kitchen, sweaty and satisfied. I could deal with my family as long as I had a place to spin my wheels.

But when I've laced up my skates, I roll right past the rink and straight to the Mortal Kombat console. I spot S. standing on the toes of his dirty Adidas, lording over his video game pulpit, jerking his joystick in ecstatic circles. I feel something like my heart lurch into my throat. I feel something like the possibility of escape. I linger near Player 2's punch buttons and hope S. will give me a playful shove before asking me to join in the game. I'm good at this one; I play it with my brother. I know most of the Friendship Fatalities, how to use Scorpion's spear to cheat (back, back, low punch), how to take your opponent by surprise with a sweeping kick, a swift uppercut to the jaw.

S.'s friends announce my arrival, but he just furrows his brow and bares his buck teeth, concentrating on the pixelated violence in front of him. A crowd forms, rapt with wonder, as S.'s avatar removes another avatar's spinal column. "Finish him!" they shout, and he happily complies, high-fiving his pals in victory. I join in and place my open palm in the fray. S.'s hand weakly meets mine and then his eyes. And when I see the dull black of his pupils, his face grimacing, I know there's nothing left here to chase. We've reached a dead end. The window in his mouth is barred shut.

✧

The game continues, round after round, with S. in the thick of the action. He continues to ignore the pathetic shape of me hovering at his side. Defeated and deflated, I skate beyond the heaving mass of seventh grade boys to conceal my blows. Maybe not tonight, but soon, S. will dump me. Or one of his friends will do it for him. I won't know whether it's the way I kiss or simply the way I am, but there will be a reason he'll never disclose. Michelle rests a hand on my shoulder with a knowing look and offers a sip of her Pepsi. I forget to remove her lipstick-stained straw and suck. All I taste is blood.

I want to tell Michelle I've shaved my legs, including the knees, but what's the point. No one can tell in this dim light anyway. Plus, she's too busy flirting with S.'s best friend, a moon-faced cutie in a Looney Tunes tee she'd never let touch her. Everyone knows she only lets Hot Chad from high school secretly finger her on park benches after school. I roll my eyes and then my wheels out to the rink, leaving my life as a wanted girl—a girl who belongs—behind.

I swerve and sway, back and forth, around and around, until my feet grow heavy, until my thighs burn and quiver. As I round each corner now, the air resists my body like a magnet repelling. It doesn't matter. I keep skating, song after song, until my legs feet toes are numb and quiet. Until all I can feel is the dull ache of my mouth. My gauze sags and shifts. It slides to the top of my palate, creeps to the base of my tongue. I try to push it back in place but end up grazing those gummy vacancies, the bitter tang of leaky battery on my lips.

My mouth is no longer crowded; there's enough room now. My teeth will straighten, the braces will be removed, and eventually I'll find a boy who takes serious notice. But as I dart between the shadowy forms of the other skaters, this thought offers no comfort. Because there's still too much space, too many places to lose ourselves and one another, to hide and to flee. Dad's crawling out of his skin; Mom is trapped in hers. And I'm still searching for a place for mine to matter. S. was a way to matter. He was a distraction, a way to skim along the surface, a way to suspend myself before I fell back into the black—that tumult of questions begging to be asked.

What will happen now? What whim will I find to fill up my time? To carry me away from the sad and the silent, away from the diseased and the dark? How long will Dad live with his parents? How long will we? And what about Her? Will she become more than a disembodied voice in our lives? And what if I want her to be more? What if I don't mind? What if I actually understand? When will Mom return home? What is home? And for how long will she live there? How long will she live at all? What will happen now? What will happen?

I round another bend and see S. in the arcade, still holding court. The Advil's worn off completely. My mouth is a throbbing wound. The DJ announces "couples skate only" and I exit the rink, breathlessly rolling to a stop. I lean my heaving body against the railing and watch the couples sail by, the breeze at their backs, the whole world open to them in a way that isn't scary or precarious. I wipe the sweat from my brow and absently lick those hollows in my mouth again. I remember what Dr. Wilson said before I left her office: *Don't poke around in the holes left behind. Forget they're there.* But it's hard to forget when the tongue reminds. When everything reminds you of what's missing. ✧

63

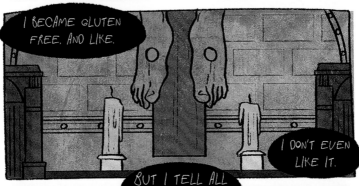

AND I DIDN'T TIP THE DELIVERY GUY.

AFTER HE WALKED UP FIVE FLIGHTS OF STAIRS TO MY APARTMENT.

...ALSO I'M STEALING WIFI FROM MY NEIGHBOR

AND I FEEL. UH. I FEEL REALLY BAD ABOUT IT.

booth

WORLD MUSIC AND ARTS FESTIVAL, SANTIAGO, CHILE

David Brunson

— for Ivana

I kicked empty tear gas canisters
through the graffitied streets

to your home, heard their hiss
in the notes you sang into the caustic air.

The city wiped the blood from its face.
After so much running, you still

danced with me, whirling faster than fear
across the park's trampled grass to crooked

fiddle reels, our boots stomping through dust
until it seemed even the fires

of far-off Caracas were extinguished.
Yes, it's true, there's so little we can fix.

So much comes out
                    torn, but I'll still play
this broken violin
                    for you.

MISS TEXAS CONSIDERS TALKING ABOUT HER TOOTH

Corey Miller

M Y SISTER, WHO BECAME MISS EL PASO and then Miss Texas, is on stage about to answer the *What would you do to change the world* question to become Miss America. She looks close to God under those hot lamps, amongst the remaining Miss States, in front of the lens that transports her image to flat-screens across the Land of the Free.

The judges ask her this question, and I know she wants to reveal her tooth, the wisdom in the back of her mouth that gave her the ability to stop eating, keeping her not detention-camp skinny, but sexy-model-on-the-cover-of-*Glamour* skinny. Not like before her tooth, when she found out she couldn't bear children and gained anxiety weight as if praying for labor.

She could answer the question by saying, "Miss Indiana's response about ending world hunger is bullshit. Only *I* can end world hunger, as I did for my family." But she'd say it in a more Miss America way. Not how us girls speak to one another at our local honky-tonk, Gringo Theory, after a bucket of Buds.

At first she thought it was smoked roadside brisket stuck in her teeth. She flossed until an iron taste salivated. She spit into her hand the bloody vitamin mixture. Over the next few days her appetite disappeared. She felt not only full but more energetic than ever. She ran across El Paso, then back. She ran to Austin, then back. Still not exhausted, she ran the border of the state, even the panhandle Texas sacrificed to Oklahoma to remain a slave state. Now she's running for Miss America.

In her application she had to prove she has never been married and is a legal US citizen. That was a long process.

She's frozen up there, mouth not moving. The judges start to converse amongst themselves. She could say, "I will undo the wrongs our country has stuck us with. To actually be human and give a shit about the ground we walk on." But she'd say it less bluntly, in more of a reassuring parent way. Some way to let America know that it can redeem itself.

She looks for me amidst the audience; I'm her dam, her full-length mirror, her coach to keep her in check. The spotlight is shining in her eyes like a policeman pulling her over for drunk driving. Without eating she gets drunk so fast.

At first she denied it when I asked whether she had stopped eating. I stalked her to catch what she was doing. I feared she was starving herself or puking to maintain that weight. Then she swallowed hard and confessed—her tooth was seeping nourishment. She opened her mouth into a pint glass. It filled with what looked like orange juice, full of pulp. I drank it and it tasted like fish oil, enough omega-3 to restart a heart. She says it tastes like holy water, a church of dirty hands.

She began feeding me every morning for breakfast, waterfalling into my mouth. We didn't need food stamps anymore and could afford our cousin's deportation lawyer.

We started canning her tooth juice like jam. When the cans weren't enough, we filled rain barrels. We could have opened a craft-local-organic-fair-trade-vegan drink business to capitalize on it, but instead we snuck it to the homeless and people we trusted. They started sprinting like their asses were on fire, ready for a revolution.

On stage she's like a robot, solid-state and perfect on the eyes. She believes if she wins she'll be able to reroute this trajectory we're on, like we'll make America great for once. She could answer by telling the truth: "My body wants to be a mother, to feed everyone and be depended upon. To not be like my sister, who sits and waits for results." She would say it in that I've-unfucked-God-for-smiting-my-womb sort of way. Not meaning to scold.

I told her the world isn't ready for this. America isn't ready for this. We abuse every little luxury we're given, like public spaces being vandalized. The government would own her. However, my sister is a glass half-full.

The other states in the running look smug in their I'm-going-to-win dresses, their blemishes hidden under bronzed cover-up, demanding to catch up to my sister's natural tan.

My sister could say what we agreed she would: "I believe in the melting pot, and I will work toward uniting the world." Something hollow, something bulletproof.

She poses up there, bucktooth smile as wide as the border, ready to regurgitate an answer. Orange drool slides down her chin and falls onto her breasts. It clashes with her outfit. I'm sitting in a river of hungry young girls who idolize her, ready to eat up every word of the next Miss America. ✧

SPLIT PORTRAIT

Jane Morton

i.
Sometimes there are two
    of us. Sometimes we are both

in the room. I am sitting still as a knife
    and she is spinning

somewhere above me. A photograph
    poked full of holes and hanging

from a string. A makeshift lure
    I bite. Every time there is blood

in the air. Every time the light
    bleeds through differently.

ii.
In the dark I drop my shape,
    my knife. Clothes tossed

on the floor. A fairy circle
    around the bed, attempted

protection. I'm always under
    the covers when I undress.

I always wait until morning
       to tidy up.

iii.
Greedy for giving, I spill
       across the bed, a wound

old as hunger, festering.
       Often, nausea. Often,

damp sheets in the morning.
       I am not a woman, but god

doesn't care. Pits me red, candy
       pulp on the tile. The bathtub,

the morning their own violence. I hold
       my own head underwater.

iv.
Every time I find another
       way home.

I find another name to call
       myself. I find

a familiar in a window. I smile
       at my reflection.

SUNNY

Allison Kade

IN THE BACK ROOM OF the wedding venue, I sat on a vintage chair at an old-fashioned writing desk. I kicked off my sparkly heels, my head tight and loose at the same time, like the overstressed coils of a grandfather clock that had partially, but not completely, burst into cuckoo-cuckoo. I lifted the fluffy mountains of tulle to rest my sweaty, sore feet on the expensive oak.

Then I opened my laptop to watch gay porn.

Drunk on my signature cocktail and adrenaline, I'd puked in the bathroom before telling Lila, my maid of honor, that I wanted to call it off. The marriage license and the signatures and even the witnesses had no magical power. They were nothing more than slips of copy paper folded over twice to fit in an envelope. I could intercept the nondenominational rabbi before he mailed the marriage certificate to the city clerk's office and then none of it would count.

He's too sunny, I said to Lila, who'd known me since college. *Like, we'll have babies and he'll always be on time for pickup and he'll make brownies for all the bake sales, but when the kids are gone, will we have anything to talk about?*

You don't even have kids yet. She held my hair as I puked mushroom polenta cakes and fish kebabs. My dress puddled around me.

If you and I were both seventy, we'd have things to talk about, I said. *Like books. Neal doesn't read.*

You want to dump your fiancé—sorry, your husband—because he doesn't read? Didn't you already know that?

Neal called me a snob when I told him on our third date that graphic novels didn't count. Then he laughed and I laughed, and we pretended that he didn't really think I was a snob and that I didn't really think he was unintellectual. After dating-not-dating Micah for almost two years, goddamn, it was a breath of fresh air how straightforward Neal was. He didn't exhaust me with the weight of the world. He took himself to the bagel shop on Sunday mornings, bought a physical newspaper, and ate an everything bagel with blueberry cream cheese while he read the comics section.

Once, he and I watched a documentary that mentioned something about Gandhi. Neal said, really vulnerably, *What exactly did Gandhi do, again?* And I told him I wouldn't judge, I couldn't, I loved him, and I rehashed a basic history about India trying to gain independence from the Brits and he asked, *The British were in India? When was that? And why?*

He liked that I went to Columbia. I was his smart girl and he was proud. I told him I didn't judge him about the Gandhi thing, but I did.

Lea pounded on the door and wanted to know whether I was OK. Out there in the banquet hall, Sarah was eating canapes with her husband and kid, her belly full with Number Two. Did I want that life for myself? With Neal?

Lila whispered that if that was what I really wanted, to un-marry Neal, then I should do it ASAP. The band was playing the "Electric Slide," and he was out on the dance floor, grinning stupidly, sliding up playfully next to his mom, a woman just as simple and loving as he. Micah was out there, too, with some girl he'd met a week earlier at Neal's bachelor party. I didn't want him at my wedding, but part of me was glad: I wanted him to watch me move on. I wanted him to see me with the charming, kind man I'd chosen to marry. I wanted to feel the contrast, to remind myself that Micah was gnarled, that I'd chosen a future of brightness and ease with Neal.

But no, I wished he hadn't come. I wasn't supposed to spend my wedding day thinking about another man.

Almost everything I know about love, I learned from an elderly man in hospice named Sunil who died last year.

Sunil came from a traditional Indian family. His relatives had disowned him when he came out as gay, except for his sister, who secretly sent him a birthday card each year. It was the seventies. They wouldn't stop talking about AIDS and didn't want to see him shrivel up and die. Sunil finally married his partner, Robert, after twenty years, when the Supreme Court let them. They had lived together for decades in a glass-paneled high rise. No kids, but lots of dinner parties. Robert's parents were more welcoming, but he and Sunil were their own family, aloft in a glass haven.

The first time I visited Sunil, he didn't mention Robert. He didn't even say he was gay, but a wall of alphabetized DVDs did the talking. *Butt-Fuck Banshees* was neatly slotted next to *The Bone Ranger*. The curated collection sat on an expensive bookshelf, facing the front door. The first thing any visitor saw was *Six Slimy Mansluts* shimmying next to *Sorest Rump*.

Sunil tended to his collection with as much care as any film connoisseur. Something about his unabashed sexuality made me uncomfortable. He offered me tea and biscuits and spoke with a kind formality. If I'd had a warm Indian grandfather who served me sweet, milky chai and chided me about whether my job was a *job* or a *career*, it would've been him.

Finally, after a month of visiting him once a week, I asked why he showcased his porn collection before anything else. Sunil was a musician, but his flute lay in a closet somewhere; he was an artist, but you had to enter all the way into the kitchen before you saw his paintings.

Alzheimer's had picked Robert apart neuron by neuron, he told me. They were the only repositories of each other's memories. As Robert evaporated, so did Sunil's only witness.

Sunil remembered a time they went skinny-dipping in early March and nearly got hypothermia. On their wedding night, after they got legally married at age sixty-five, they rented out the diviest bar they could find. They invited not just their friends but all the gay people they could find, come to Off the Wagon, free drinks all night, so they could educate the young gay kids who drank their liquor: *This is what love looks like. Don't let the new laws fool you, you've still got to know how to fight for each other.*

But those times had flowed out of Robert's brain as if it were an oversaturated sponge. A few years later, the young gays who came for free booze probably didn't remember the two old guys footing the bill. Sunil constantly worried that he'd falter for just a moment and his life with Robert would disappear entirely. The flute, the paintings, those were vestiges of Sunil. But the porn—it was a symbol of his love for his dead husband.

Their whole last year together, he and Robert spent hours a day watching porn on their flat-screen. Even when Robert no longer knew Sunil's name or his own, the two lovers clenched hands and watched men with large cocks whip each other. *It seemed to remind him of who he was*, Sunil said. *He bought most of these DVDs.*

In the early days of frontal lobe atrophy, Robert became hypersexual. He'd walk into a bakery, and a baguette would give him an erection. He had sex with Sunil five times a day, which made Sunil sob because it was the beginning of the end. He would cover his lover's back in tears. As the disease ate away his brain, Robert lost the concepts of sex and gender. Still, he seemed to find solace in sitting with Sunil, holding hands, watching strange men ravage one another.

After a few months of chai and biscuits, I asked Sunil, *Do you want to watch something?*

You would do that for me? He gathered our crumb-strewn plates.

I'd watched porn once or twice with a guy I dated briefly in college, but we hadn't watched *together*. More like he watched Hot Slut Number Three coo about the lead's cock and then waited for me to imitate her.

In this sleek apartment, I felt drawn to the cheesy titles and the neon images on the DVD box covers. Mostly, I was drawn to Sunil's love for Robert.

Lila and I agreed that I should take a beat to calm down and make sure I didn't need to puke again. I retreated to the ready room, where a professional had painted my face only a few hours earlier.

With my parents in the banquet hall—so happy, the last of their daughters married off like in some biblical fairy tale—I assured Lea through the door that I'd be fine. I whispered to Lila that I needed to be alone for a sec, and she reluctantly left me. Then I found my laptop in the suitcase I'd packed for the hotel.

When I stole the DVDs from Sunil's apartment and uploaded the files to my hard drive, I considered hiding them in some orifice of my computer, some folder labeled "Taxes" or "Admin." Instead, I saved them to my desktop in a folder called "KINKY GAY PORN." My own bookcase at the front of the house.

I kept waiting for Neal to find it. If he did, he never said anything. More likely, he'd never snooped on my computer. He liked everything bright and clear and out in the open. Why would he snoop? Neal didn't have any dark, moldy parts of his personality. I'd been furious when Micah broke up with me, screamed at him, "What do you mean it's for my own good?"

Micah would have found the folder. Maybe he would have renamed it to let me know he'd been there. Something coy, like "Is There Something I Should Know?" or "Do You Want to Try This?" Micah might've left a whip in the bed as a joke that wasn't a joke, like that time he dripped hot candle wax on my nipples and I laughed because it kind of tickled but also it was hot as hell and he slipped his finger inside me and I came three times that night.

If Neal watched porn, he probably watched vanilla stuff, girls with big boobs, maybe a couple of threesomes. But I didn't know for sure. He was the kind of guy who'd never admit his porn habits to me because it wasn't proper. Everything in its right place. That's why I was drunk on blackberry whiskey lemonade and sick on miniature turkey sliders. How could I have a normal life with someone so normal?

Our sex was enjoyable, but it wasn't the biting, tearing kind. It never felt *dirty*. I always felt guilty after sleeping with Micah. Maybe it was the secrecy at the beginning of our relationship. It was different with Neal. He and I made love. And I loved that. Neal supported me, cheered for me unconditionally, admired me. Was being basic really so bad? He was one of the kindest people I'd ever met, like he stopped for homeless people on his way to work, even if he saw ten of them, even if he was tired.

I'd started volunteering with hospice after my grandma passed away because I felt bad that I'd traveled down to Florida only a handful of times to see her. Hospice was part of a campaign I was waging to overcome my self-centeredness. Some people are born thinking of others, like my sister Lea. Her impulse was to tend to others, whereas growing up I used to protest when anyone asked me to share a bite of my food. Something bad would happen, like a friend would skin his knee on the playground, and my first thought would be for my own wellbeing. I'd have to remind myself to inquire whether that friend was all right, that I should ask a teacher for a Band-Aid. At some point when I was a teenager, I decided that focusing on others was a learned behavior. I practiced waiting a few beats in a conversation before inserting myself. I asked about others even when I didn't feel like it. At first I felt like an impostor, but it grew into habit. Still, there were times it'd creep in. I couldn't fully shake that kneejerk impulse.

When my grandmother was dying, I was in the thick of my non-relationship with Micah. Then she died and I realized that I'd done it again. As penance, I signed up as a hospice volunteer.

Micah praised my volunteer work but in a removed, ironic way. He asked for interesting stories from my visits, tried to get at the kernel of why I felt compelled to do it. He'd want to talk about my emotions, about the existential nature of the work, about the value of comforting old people when they were going to die— really, what was the point of being kind to a young person, either, since they were going to die too? What was the point of any of this? I liked that about him, the fact that he never let me get by with a superficial answer to anything. But I also just wanted to do my volunteer work and feel good about it, end of story.

By the time I met Neal, my grandmother had been dead for four years. I was considering quitting hospice. If I'd signed up out of grandmother guilt, when was payment rendered? I was tired.

Multiple old people had died on me by then. Ricardo was a seventy-something Venezuelan man who wore a suit whenever I came over. We played chess until the clock hit seven and he joked he was turning into a pumpkin. I visited him for a year and a half before cancer took him.

Sandra died after only three months, and toward the end she mostly slept when I was there. I hung out with her Jamaican nurse, and we ate spiced beef patties together. I ran into the nurse a few months after Sandra died, at a CVS, and she told me that Sandra had appeared to her as a ghost, and I said that made sense because she was basically a ghost when I knew her, too.

I told all of this to Neal. He didn't believe in ghosts, he said, and I hated that irrationally unblinking rationality. But then he told me to keep volunteering, and even offered to go with me sometimes, if that was allowed, which it wasn't. He said maybe he'd take on a hospice commission of his own, to support me. That's when I told him I loved him. I liked who he helped me become. That week, I reached out to my program coordinator and was assigned to Sunil.

I tried to break up with Neal once, when we'd been dating for half a year. That whole time, I'd felt this conviction that there was *more* to him. Maybe sunniness was just a mask to hide his fatalism about the state of our world. He'd tell me stories from his day, like, a client came in and would you believe that he'd groomed his dog to match his own outfit? That would be the whole story. Neal would always stop short of the negative. On the rare occasion he spoke ill of someone, he always berated himself afterward and felt guilty about it for days.

He hated sarcasm, and who hates sarcasm? But then, every so often, after I'd decided he wasn't funny and maybe that was all right, not everyone needs to be a comedian, he'd drop a joke bomb and I'd really laugh, from my belly and through my ribs, half out of humor and half out of surprise.

When I said the words, *I don't know if this is working, I don't know if we're intellectually compatible,* his eyes watered. I did love him. It wrenched me to see him sad, an emotion that just didn't fit him. I'd tried the dark and pessimistic route with Micah, and it hadn't worked. We'd talk politics and I'd fall into a funk about the decline of democracy; we'd talk religion and come to the conclusion that there was no God and that we were praying to the false gods of health and wellness and politics in an effort to fill the gaping hole in our souls. I'd try to support Micah emotionally with his sister Frankie, but he'd bark at me because he was under stress and I'd clap back at him and both of us would cry because Frankie's life was unfair and we didn't know how to fix it.

Micah was right, in the end. I didn't belong with someone so much like myself. I did deserve someone warm, someone who'd lift me up. I loved the omigosh-can-I-have-one expression Neal made when we passed a puppy. I loved Neal. I just wasn't sure

I knew him, or that there was more to know. After dating him for a while, I'd find myself about to gossip about a friend or a coworker. But then I wouldn't. I'd think about his reluctance to speak ill of anyone. I'd feel myself being stretched by him, let myself be pushed toward my better impulses.

Those were the times I'd think, OK, there's got to be a *there* there. Maybe, in the end, Neal had a more nuanced take on human nature than I did. Maybe he observed far more than he let on. Maybe his perspective on the world was so intuitive and kaleidoscopic that he thought it was obvious. Maybe he was too shy to tell me he was a submissive, that he wanted me to make him my slave. Maybe he had a mommy thing he wanted to act out.

I tried to explain this to him. He thought I was joking about making him my slave, so I went along with it and laughed, too.

I didn't break up with Neal at that six-month conversation. During that talk he got serious, and I thought, maybe that's all I need. To know that he has depth of feeling. I like the sun. You don't go to the beach for the clouds. I just wanted to know that, when the situation called for it, he could also provide shade.

For a year, I visited Sunil once a week. He'd make me sweet chai and set out biscuits, and then we'd sit side by side on his leather couch to watch whatever DVD I chose.

We started with basic bondage—buff men skin-slicked into rubber bodysuits, ball gags shoved into mouths, ropes that burned through captives' wrists. We moved on to cock-and-ball torture, fist-fucking, electrical stimulation, piss play. I'd brush biscuit crumbs from my lips as an actor inserted his fist into another man's anus, striving, until his limb was swallowed by another human's innards, all the way to the shoulder, allowing him to swim among his partner's guts, because if that boiling, sweaty stew isn't who we are deep inside, what is?

The first time we watched, Sunil waited forty-five minutes before cautiously unzipping his fly. I didn't say anything, just sipped my chai, as he snuck a look at me and then gingerly ran a finger along his cock.

Most people don't assume that when you say *hospice volunteer* you mean *watch porn with an old guy who masturbates next to you*. Despite the strange kindredness of my relationship with Sunil, saying it out loud felt rapey, though I'm not sure who people would think was taking advantage of whom.

I didn't think Neal would understand what I had with Sunil. I didn't either, not really.

Weeks passed. As men affixed weights to stretch each other's balls and bashed each other's testicles with paddles, Sunil quietly jacked off next to me, his face a mix of pleasure and nostalgia. One time I tried masturbating, too, snaking a finger into my jeans and under my panty line. He didn't say anything as I tried to turn myself on, as he rhythmically pleasured himself up and down a few paces to my right, and I was grateful. Even after he came, driblets of semen sticking to the curly gray hairs on his inner thigh, I wasn't close at all. Despite my fascination with the men who acted as puppies to shed the weight of their personhood, it wasn't really sexual for me. I just thought it was beautiful how these men pretended they were dogs and no one judged them.

Aside from that one failed attempt at turning myself on, I just watched quietly with Sunil so he, too, could be seen and not judged.

We were watching a scene with nipple torture when I noticed how large one of Sunil's testicles had grown, just the left one. It wasn't a surprise, really—hospice had told me about his testicular cancer. One day a few weeks after that, he didn't unzip his fly but still wanted to watch. So we sat together, thinking about virility and mortality. Actors on the screen played out corporal punishment. Sunil's hands rested on a pillow over his lap, trembling slightly.

The next time he bared himself to me, his left scrotum was an empty sack. We didn't talk about it. He asked me about work. What was the latest with the woman who kept stealing my lunch from the fridge? How was my mom's visit last week? What were my thoughts on wedding colors? Bridesmaids? Sunil had loved planning his wedding with Robert. Married life was the best, he said, don't let anyone get you down with that ball-and-chain shit. They're just assholes. Oh, and had I decided what to get Neal for his birthday? Sunil had several nice whiskey recommendations; I'd said he was a whiskey man, right?

Then we watched men use wires to electrocute each other. They screamed mawkishly in pain-delight.

Over the next few weeks, Sunil's face grew thinner.

One man took a comically tremendous penis into his mouth and slid it down his throat, deep, without gagging. Sunil wheezed as he orgasmed, and sometimes coughed up bloody sputum.

Toward the end, he started falling asleep. He'd be half awake when I arrived, a radiation ghost, and sometimes he didn't even make it through the opening scene. I'd finish the videos for him, making myself watch, his hand no longer touching himself but instead grasping mine.

The only family member to attend his funeral was his sister, but his non-Indian friends researched Hindu burial rituals online. We wore white, casual clothes. It was an open casket, and his body was covered with loads of flowers. His ashes were strewn in Central Park. Someone had read somewhere that Hindu tradition included a feast on the twelfth or thirteenth day after the funeral. We gathered in Sunil's empty apartment in the sky, which would be sold afterward so the profits could be donated to a charity for LGBTQ youth. Someone had brought samosas from an Indian restaurant, and I ate one as I walked around the glassed-in living room one last time.

I'd known he was dying. I wouldn't have met him if he weren't. But his death didn't feel like Ricardo's or Sandra's. I missed Sunil deeply. He showed me what it meant to love fully and unflinchingly. Not just in the way he loved Robert, but in the way he loved me. I aspired to love Neal in that way. I thought maybe Neal already did love me like that, or as nearly as he could.

I hoped Sunil didn't visit me as a ghost, like Sandra with her nurse. If he did, maybe he would show up with cookies and chai, or a DVD.

His friends, mostly older gay men, didn't glance twice at the DVD wall. I was the only person under thirty-five, and one of only two women. When no one was looking, I slipped one of my favorite DVDs into my messenger bag. Then I said what the hell and shoveled in all the DVDs that would fit, the ball gags and the piss-drinkers and the floggers and the men who acted like puppies. Guests stared, but I grabbed everything I could and hurried into the hallway and down the elevator and onto the street before anyone could stop me.

My feet were up on the desk in the back room of the wedding hall in Cobble Hill, my sparkly heels were on the floor, and my eyes were bleeding tears and mucus and regrets. A man dominated another man with a cat-o-nine-tails whip while, in the banquet room, my cousins pecked at hors d'oeuvres and my parents showed off the cha-cha they'd learned from ballroom dancing lessons.

Neal slid into the dark room and hovered by the door. I didn't wait for him to ask what I was doing. I turned my laptop toward him.

The submissive groaned while the dom cracked a whip.

I guess I wanted Neal to do the work for me. The kink, the domination, the pain—it picked at a dark knot of something inside people. Inside me. This video would bounce against his sunny armor. *Ha. What's that.* He'd find it funny, or pretend to. He'd discount it as something for deviants. He wouldn't be able to dispel the mental image, at least of me watching it. *Debauchery,* he'd think, and he'd consider me debaucherous, and not in the fun way. He'd say, well, I guess that'll be an annulment.

But instead, he pulled up the chair. We finished the video. I got angry at first, thinking my attempt to scare him off had gone over his head. But he wasn't that dense. He was the sun, and the sun shone on everything indiscriminately. When the video ended, as if to make a point, I chose a different file. Halfway through, he reached for my hand. I thought of Sunil and Robert, holding hands and watching porn till the end.

When I didn't feel like watching anymore, I turned it off.

Neal kept holding my hand, then led me back into the light. ✧

MOM, WHEN I CALLED

Taylor Kirby

the police
      for your ever
-black eye, I did so
      knowing *at least*
40% of cops
      have made crime scenes
and cover-ups
      of the bodies
that share their beds.
      That's like asking
the fire department
      to save your home
when three out of five
      hoses spray water &
the others punish flames
      with gasoline.
Mom,
      are you still burning?

SOUL TO KEEP

Rochelle Hurt

Goodman—You have opened skulls and dissected the human fœtus. Have you ever, in these dissections, discovered any appearance of a soul? (Voltaire, "The Study of Nature")

Argument for Keeping the Soul[i] in the Forearm:
Soul as tender fish belly[ii], soul as knife-tease[iii], soul as scannable tracking device[iv].

---

[i] I never actually said this prayer before bed, but I knew it, and it came to me the first time I was put under anesthesia, along with a question—not *if*, but *where*. Hopefully not the part of me the surgeon was about to remove.

[ii] *Me*—that is: twenty-two, F; diagnosis of papillary thyroid cancer; history of untreated depression and self-harm.

iii Scars evident on left forearm; presents with no clinical symptoms at time of diagnosis; *denies pain*, as one doctor wrote in my medical chart.

iv My journal, day of diagnosis: *Irony—the depressive begs to live.* Then a bunch of poems about God's indifference. In the pages after that, God and Death both vanish.

Argument for Keeping the Soul in the Nostril[v]:

Soul as proximal pocket, snot locket, breath filter. Never the left one, though—*right hand of* and all that.

v I had a perpetually infected nose ring, so I came to my college art classes with a Band-Aid on my face to hide the pus and blood. To cover the cuts on my arm, I wore long-sleeved shirts. Learning of the nose ring beneath the Band-Aid, a professor said: *Ah, vanity.* I don't know whether she was referring to the decorative metal that was eating my tissue away, or my refusal to remove it.

Argument for Keeping the Soul in the Appendix[vi]:

The question of whether the soul has a purpose remains unanswered for me. While some might point out that there has been no evidence to date that the soul has a physiological function in the same way that, for example, the lung's function is to respirate, the heart's is to circulate blood, and the bowel's is to digest food, others might contend that the true purpose of the soul, vestigial or otherwise, has simply yet to be (re)discovered.

vi I'd never been to the hospital before age twenty-two. No appendicitis, no allergic reactions, no stitches or broken bones.

Argument for Keeping the Soul in the Genitals:

Insofar as we hide, fear, flaunt, loathe, prune, shield, desire, identify with, and revere them, maybe we already do. Sex as spiritual: open my little window[vii].

[vii] Three phone calls in a row: To the doctor, who repeated the word from his voicemail—suspicious—and said surgery would be scheduled for next month; to a crush, who said *Yeah!* when I asked him out; and to my mother, who said nothing for a long time after I told her what the doctor had said. In the weeks leading up to surgery, I would have the best sex of my then-life, which seemed suddenly shorter than before.

Argument for Keeping the Soul in the Ear[viii]:

Long ago, people knew of a sound made by the soul that mimics the sound of its original source (think conch shell, or Pikachu, the squirrelly yellow Pokémon that says only variations of its own name). This soul-sound was an aural peephole into the divine that, unlike full, obliterative exposure to the divine, offered itself in a form bearable to the human body and mind. It was audible only when a bodily orifice was held very close to the ear, but it was considered rude to listen to one's soul without offering your own, so at religious ceremonies (and, I imagine, in bedrooms) people sat very quietly ear to ear.

Eventually the sounds of industry and church organs drowned out the sound of souls, and people forgot the sound existed—until an ancient text was found that appeared to translate the soul through musical measures. After this discovery, metaphysical scholars spent centuries trying to create a device through which this sound might once again be heard, a sort of spiritual phonograph. Designs ranged from the extravagant (contraptions involving speculums, pulleys, ball weights, funnels, and waxed string) to the absurd (think *Honey, I Shrunk the Kids*) to the obscene (essentially a speaker hooked up to a colostomy bag). But what better contraption to access the soul's register than the human ear itself? The last known scholar of soul audiology was found on the floor of his laboratory missing both his ears. An autopsy showed one ear partially digested in his stomach and one caught in his esophagus. The cause of death, however, was a massive heart attack with ventricular rupture—*completely obliterated* was how the medical examiner described it.

---

viii When they put me under, sound was the last sense to go. Suspended without light or gravity, I could hear my gurney being rolled into a new space. Beeping and clanging and chatter. The doctor's voice close to my ear when he said, "You don't do this anymore, right?" When I woke, I realized he was referring to the scars on my arm.

Argument for Keeping the Soul in the Mouth[ix]:

Texture would be a nice touch: are you crunchy or smooth, grainy or lumpy, a tongueful of pulp, cotton, or ash?

---

ix While accidental swallowing might be a concern, there is no reason to believe the soul could actually be digested. Many things pass right through. When I swallowed a Barbie shoe, my mother swears, the pink plastic reappeared in my diaper the same day, nearly pristine. Twenty years later, when I was given morphine after my first surgery, the chicken broth I vomited up was the same color and consistency it had been going in. Three minutes inside me and these traces of another animal remained unchanged.

Argument for Keeping the Soul in the Throat[x]:
   God's little gag[xi].

_____

[x] When removing a thyroid gland from the throat, the surgeon must be careful to peel away the tiny parathyroid glands, to gingerly reposition them if disturbed. Often they bruise during surgery but heal after a few weeks in their newly empty thyroid bed.

[xi] Two weeks after my thyroidectomy, I found a lump in my neck. Metastasis to the lymph nodes—fairly common. *How did we miss it?* a receptionist asked while scheduling my next surgery.

Argument for Keeping the Soul in the Spleen:
   Ease of removal.[xii]

_____

[xii] *Out in a jiff,* the surgeon had said—*thyroidectomies are easy.* The second time, they went in through the same incision and pulled out a string of lymph nodes like pearls. My great-grandmother's superstition: always arrive and leave through the same door.

Argument for Keeping the Soul in the Blood:
   Bodily *duende*[xiii]. The sacred as rhythm. A kind of coursing.
   Course as in path. As in a series of lessons. A getting toward
   better. And if not? Then a little soul-letting. Or souls treated
   with leeches. Soul transfusions[xiv]. Vampiric theology. Soul
   gore and soul slasher movies. Is that such a bad thing? The
   soul stained with corporeality.

_____

[xiii] I once had a poetry professor who, on the first day of class, handed out a list of words never to use in a poem. *Soul,* he said, was the worst offense.

[xiv] Donations and transfusions might be a concern, sure, but perhaps a little soul-sharing would be helpful in cultivating empathy. In my split hospital

room, I shared the air with a faceless girl. We breathed in tandem over the curtain as our blood ferried oxygen to our organs and filtered each other's carbon dioxide out through our mouths. Her lips on my breath, her breath touched by my blood. Our matching neck scars. The room a body we lived in.

Argument for Keeping the Soul in the Frontal Lobe of the Brain: Paradoxically, this argument presupposes a metaphysical schema that separates spirit from intellect but strives to reunite them[xv]. Something beyond Cartesian dualism of body and spirit—the true human form trisected but waiting for the sacred glue that would offer unity at last.

[xv] In Catholic school, the concept of the Holy Trinity, wherein the Father, the Son, and the Holy Spirit were not equal to one another but were all equal to God, seemed like an algebra equation, which explains either my aversion to religion or my aversion to math. However, the notion that body, mind, and spirit were all different and yet all *me* was easy—though after my thyroid gland and lymph nodes were removed, this seemed less accurate. Where was I now—inside myself or sitting in a heap of medical waste? Maybe both, until they incinerated the smaller bits of *me*.

Addendum—Options for Keeping the Soul Outside the Body: I. In the Refrigerator[xvi xvii xviii].

[xvi] My mother keeps condiments well past their expiration dates in her fridge—even mayo. The mustard, at least, seems to keep for years beyond its stamp.

[xvii] In preparation for radioactive iodine treatment after both surgeries, I adhered to a low-iodine diet—no iodized salt, no dairy, no fish, no salted or processed food. Everything from scratch. My mother made forty individually packaged servings of approved meals for me. Sentimental, I kept the labels on the Tupperware for months after they were emptied and reused. Keepsakes.

[xviii] Or the freezer—surely many await the marriage of theology and cryogenics.

II. Cupboards, Closets[xix], Drawers[xx], or Shelves[xxi].

[xix] My teen bedroom is now a guest room in my mother's house, the evidence of my adolescence stored in the closet: patchwork purse, chunky heels, school uniform skirt, sketchpads, dried out Lip Smackers, highlighted bible.

[xx] I always kept my cutting razors in a drawer, organized by size, which helped in a lot of ways. But the biggest scar came from surgery, and after that, cutting seemed somewhat pointless. Without it, I felt no better or worse.

[xxi] Upon death, the memorial shrine a mother might make is pre-set.

III. In an HVAC System[xxii xxiii xxiv].

[xxii] Air return: *soul* into *spirit* into *suspire* into *breath*.

[xxiii] Visiting my mom after some time recovering, I was kept up all night by the vent in my room—some piece of debris rattling incessantly against the grate. I never heard it before or after.

[xxiv] So that your house breathes you in and out, so that you may become a fine dust settling silently over everything.

IV. In a Glove Compartment[xxv xxvi xxvii].

[xxv] Soul as a valid form of ID.

[xxvi] Soul as contraband. I found my razors in my old art supplies at my mother's house and snuck them out, intending to throw them away discreetly. Forgotten, they remained in my car for over a year.

[xxvii] Soul-flare in case of emergency. After blood tests showed residual disease despite two surgeries and radiation therapy, I spent a lot of time in my car, screaming.

V. In the Garden[xxviii xxix xxx].

[xxviii] Potential for growth, given rain and sunlight.

[xxix] Potential for reincarnation, given a hungry enough bird, rabbit, or squirrel.

[xxx] Potential for rest, though not necessarily eternal. I once saw a gravestone that said: *Just Waiting.* ✧

SISTERS SHARING A PILLOW, OR, "THANK YOU, 117 LOMIA"

A. Prevett

I am not the best lesbian. I don't say this
        because of what rests between.
                I mean astrology is beyond me.
I'm a December baby,
        Sagittarius. I know this.
                But that's all I have.
The rising, the set.
        The moment
                I went from one cell   to two?
I can't name it.
        My chart is incomplete. And so, we add this to
                my list of not-accomplishments, alongside
graduating and coming out to the kind couple
        who run the corner store
                and sometimes compliment my nails.
117 Lomia, too, has compliments to give.
        Cute socks, she says.
                Good job getting up
before noon. Those jeans are out of your world.
        She hovers in my constellation. We share it
                like sisters sharing a pillow
in the back seat as their father drives home
        from grandmother's wake.
                In this, my most pathetic fallacy, 117
clasps our grief between
        our palms, as if to diamond
                our sad coal. This makes sense: Lomia
is the older sister here. Lomia:
        for thousands, millions of years, lingering.
                Watching over.
Oh, Lomia: care for me, care.

A Conversation with

s a m   s a x

by Abby Johnson

sam sax is a queer, Jewish poet and educator. They are the author
of two collections, *madness* and *bury it*. The latter won the 2017
James Laughlin Award from the Academy of American Poets.
They are a Wallace Stegner Fellow at Stanford University.

De During their visit to Butler University in 2019 as part of
the Vivian S. Delbrook Visiting Writers Series, sax talked with
Booth about grieving within exploitative systems, the form of
diasporic writing, and the name of their future pet pig.

ABBY JOHNSON: You've talked about how the diasporic elements of your identity play a role in your content. Could you talk about how those elements play a role in the form of your work, either performed or on the page?

sam sax: In my second book there's a poem called "Diaspora" where there are large caesuras between longer fragmented sentences, and there's a lot of space between lines in the poem. I think that's the most concrete attempt to show both the continuity and fracture in Jewish diaspora. So it's part of a whole object but also in pieces and scattered.

There are those more formal, procedural ways of making poems. But this is something I've been talking about a lot because it offers an alternative to Zionism, right? That we are a diasporic people grounded in books and stories instead of a country. So I think what is most of interest and value about our people is our mutability, our survival, and our adaptability, and how, through that, we've held on to a single narrative. So writing as a Jewish person is always writing about diaspora, whether or not it's explicit in the work

AJ: You've described your work as always trying to write from "where the body meets the world." In relation to that, have you seen your work change as your relationship with your body has changed? If so, how?

ss: It's hard to know what it is exactly that changes it, whether it's just having seriously been writing for fifteen years. I don't know if it's more my relationship with my body than it is moving cities or being thirty or living with a partner for the first time.

But the thing I'm loving most is that, as I age, work that I didn't find urgent or relevant when I was younger has shifted. As I've aged, work that once read to me as corny or too quiet has opened up in new ways linked with changes I've gone through. I've started believing less that if I don't like something, the piece of writing is "bad," and more that I'm not in the place in my life to read it.

Or perhaps something about my relationship with graduate school and poetry. I came up in slam, and then in graduate school the main note I got was that I didn't need to be so explicit and that I could trust my reader more, which led to a lot of poems that are a bit more abstruse, or intentionally elusive, which in some ways opened up possibilities for meaning-making in the poem and in other ways obscured the thing that I wanted to say plainly. So the main tension I've been feeling is how much to put on the page, what is trusting a reader and what is keeping them out of what is important in the poem.

And as far as my relationship with my body, I'm having a lot less scary and unprotected sex with strangers, so that's shifted. I think then the poems are more about, not nostalgia, but reckoning with a time where I put my body more at risk, instead of the immediacy of living inside of that experience. But I think it's also clocking my body as I move through different spaces, like what it means to put my body in certain spaces.

AJ: And in the same way, do you see your work changing as your relationship with the world changes?

SS: What's the difference, right? When I was young, I had a lot of very self-righteous, utopian ideas about the world. That was my first mode of poem-making, and then it moved into self-hatred, implicating the self in harm, trying to work through the nuances of how I have received and reproduced harm.

And now I think I'm back in that utopian mindset. Or just wanting to imagine a world where my friends are able to be alive. You know, even though I don't necessarily see us surviving impending climate collapse, I am enjoying loving the people I love now, while we're alive. And so the main shift has been a radical re-orientation to the present rather than to some idea of what a future might be like.

AJ: You bring an urgency to language, history, and the history of language in *bury it* while also engaging in wordplay. I think this is a constant in your work, both performance and page. Can you talk about when in your career you saw yourself leaning into this strength of your voice?

SS: The more I've studied and spent time with language, the more it opens up to me. That's the thing I like to say about poetry, that the more I've studied it, the stranger and larger and more unknowable it's become. How that ties to etymology, in particular, has a lot to do with my shift toward Jewish diasporic understanding. Even our language has a history. It has moved like we've moved, across borders and through war, famine, and violence.

If I was stuck in a poem, the shift would always be to look at the moment where I'm stuck and look at the history of it, whether it's an object or a particular word, and let that be a door the poem can move through. That happened so much I ended up making this poem called "Etymology," which is about the history of gun violence, and it posits all these false origins for the word gun. That was in *Guernica* a while ago.

AJ: I'm also interested in humor as a device in your work. You've talked about humor as a tool to trick people into listening to you. And I'm wondering how wordplay and humor coincide. Do you think they're the same movement in your work, or do they feel different to you?

SS: I think it's easier to be funny at a poetry reading than elsewhere because everyone has a really low expectation, in general, for what is going to happen, and no one really expects humor. I don't think I could ever do stand-up, but I love bantering between poems. It's something I learned from the slam, where you have three minutes to say a thing, and here's how you pull a listener in, here's how you get them to listen to you, and now you can say the thing that you need to tell them. So that's a structure that always seeps into my writing, even when I try to push against it. And there are a lot of ways to do that. Wordplay can be one of them, especially if it's silly. The whole range of human experience has a place inside the poem.

AJ: I'm interested in the structures of your collections and how they come about. For example, the bridges in *bury it*, the erasures in *madness*, or the monster suit in "Guide to Undressing Your Monsters." It seems like that may be very important for your work or process, to have something throughout the collection that orients it toward one idea.

SS: First I think about what I would want most as a reader—what is going to keep me in a book. I think having these signposts is always really useful to me. That's also why I like books with hella section breaks. I like the opportunity to put something down, breathe, and then be pulled back into the book despite myself, which is what I hope the section break does.

It's also how I write, generally. I mean, I don't have any concrete processes, but in general if there's something I don't understand I'll write a suite of poems about it, or poems with that same title over and over again to see the various ways I can get at and analyze a particular poem. *Gay Boys and the Bridges Who Love Them* was going to be the title of *bury it*, and there were thirty poems I wrote about that. A lot of the ones that didn't make it into the book were news clippings that I reorganized or personal anecdotes of a friend who had jumped off the Golden Gate Bridge.

I think about it like Cubism. You're looking at a three-dimensional object on a flat surface, and writing in sequence is a way of turning that object to see all the various ways you can look at it and distort the thing itself. That's sequentially the footholds in a book.

AJ: There's a lot of conversation in the poetry community about poetic ancestors, whether those be historical or contemporary poets. Who are your poetic ancestors, and in what way does their work speak to yours?

SS: There are the folks who first permissioned me to make poems and challenged me to push my work in different directions, and then there are the people that I learned later were supposed to be my poetic ancestors, who in some ways were, who affected the people who I read that affected me but who weren't primary sources for me.

I read "Howl" in high school, which was the first time I read a queer Jewish person be filthy in a poem. And I've fought against the Ginsberg connection for a while, because he was not the best guy in a lot of ways, but also pretty remarkable. I came across a book by Essex Hemphill called *Ceremonies* when I was a sophomore in college, and that really transformed how I thought about what is possible in a poem. I mean, it's mostly queer men. But Audre Lorde's essays were really formative for me. That someone could have such a nuanced and visionary politic, that shows up in both the essays and the poems. *Crush* by Richard Siken was a big book for me also.

A lot of writers in the slam world were big for me as well. Before I was reading poetry seriously, I was listening and being transformed by people's stories and craft as I got to go from city to city. I think now I've started to draw further back connections to other sad, quiet homosexuals like Hart Crane.

AJ: And those are the people you "should have been reading"?

SS: I think that's it, who I've learned is in my family.

AJ: And I'm sure, like you said, in slam and local artists doing punk house stuff alongside you. A mixture of all those things.

SS: It's really been the people I'm around, that I'm closest to, that have affected my writing the most. But that's not a poetic ancestor, it's a kinship—kindred spirits pushing me and pulling from their various traditions. There were a handful of people in college doing weird, experimental, multi-disciplinary stuff that I saw and was like, "I want to do that. I want to do that with you." And then I read books on historical performance art and books of experimental monologues that were really impactful to me when I was in college. Like Kathy Acker, Adrian Piper,

Karen Finley, and folks. But it depends what day it is whose impact is most clear or how I'm thinking about it.

AJ: There's a question that every poet is getting now. As a poet working during the Trump administration, do you see the responsibility of the poet changing? And, if so, in what ways?

SS: I don't think it's any different. I think it's caused certain people to awaken to what's always been there. Not that there's an obligation for every poet to explicitly speak to the moment they're living in. That is the work I am most interested in. But poetry can be and do nearly anything, so when we talk about poets having a singular responsibility or obligation, I disagree. It's hard because every poem has politics, is a political poem, right? You can read any poem in that way. The poems that I have loved most are polemical while also having a deep, urgent sense of self. That well predates Trump; some of my favorite poets were writing in the twenties. But that's not to say that times aren't dire, and more dire for a lot of people. And that we're not on a trajectory toward annihilation. And it's important to contextualize that within a wider scope of capitalist, consumer-based harm and violence and neoliberalism. I think the myth of Trump being an anomaly instead of a product of that is dangerous in our work and how we talk about our work.

AJ: I absolutely agree. As far as *bury it*, you've talked about it as a work reckoning with the deaths of queer people and how those deaths are publicized. How do you reckon with that publicity as a queer person who is writing elegies?

ss: "Politics of Elegy" points to that difficulty. Hieu Minh Nguyen and Danez Smith and I all wrote poems with that title, and for me the moment in the poem is the sort of etymological bent: "eulogy from the greek means praise / praise from the latin means price." Praising the dead is a performance for the living and has often been a monetized process. And to reckon with being compensated for mourning, it's something I can't really get my head around.

The ways in which it provides relief for people, the writer, myself, and the ways in which it benefits from destructive capitalism felt important to talk about in the book. But I also didn't want to not grieve the people I felt I needed to grieve. I think poetry often offers a place for the nuanced, complicated politic and experiential relationship of living through unspeakably violent and political times while also holding on to joy and care inside your body. So ferrying back and forth between those two spaces is something I think poems can help us navigate, if not understand.

AJ: What boundaries do you set for yourself, or what self-care do you do, as someone whose job is living in this headspace of reckoning with grief and trauma and systemic violence?

ss: Therapy has been really useful. Sometimes after a reading folks will talk to me, or on social media or whatever, about experiences I've written about, particularly my own experiences with trauma or familial violence. Often how I've crafted and put it in a poem is the extent to which I'm trying to talk about it.

I often feel compelled to talk to people if they care about my writing since it's such a privilege, honor, and gift, but I also want to be able to say "I can't talk to you about whatever x is"—

and finding ways to set a boundary around that. Exercising and eating better have been helping. I was writing a book that was going to be about the Anthropocene and queer joy, and during my research I had a bit of a breakdown, so I put that book aside and stopped working on it. Trying to be sensitive to where my limits are is very critical.

AJ: Given that your next book is about pigs, literally and figuratively, if you owned a pig, what would you name it?

SS: An ex and I talked about owning a pig together when we were in college. There's a poem in the book about it. They wanted to call it Rainbow Queen Encyclopedia, so that name has always stuck with me. I think it'd be a cute name for a little pig baby. I want a pig and I want a pit bull and I want them to be best friends. I hope to, at some point in my life, be in a stable enough position to own and care for a pig properly.

AJ: Who are you reading right now?

SS: Right now I'm rereading Alexander Chee's collection of essays *How to Write an Autobiographical Novel.* I've got this Amos Oz book called *Jews and Words.* I just read Aria Aber's first collection, called *Hard Damage,* which is a really phenomenal book. I have Hanif [Abdurraqib]'s new book, *A Fortune for Your Disaster,* in my bag too, which is really stunning. So those are the four books I'm currently eating, and then—and this is kind of dweeby—I'm reading a couple pages of *Ulysses* every morning. ◇

under bridges

Emilie Collyer

in the chat bar / the trolls are worried / about the women / on the panel / *are the women married* / they ask / *and do they have* / *children* / *if not* / *is this the reason* / *they are so lonely?* / and need to write feminist—

in the news picture / they are four people / men in suits / nice pinstripe suits / the article points out / posing together / for a photo / the way a rock band / might have / in the 1980s / and they are / the political future / so the story says / of—

on social media / a person missing / becomes / a body found / Twitter floods / with bro- / ken ♥ / the person's body didn't always fit / but they found a way to trans-late / now gone / transmission fin—

a body / excited / erects an attack on a body that / didn't always / rides / the blowout / and / a body / exhausted / from always alert / being looked at / surrenders / to the blows of—

is that a man or a woman / one of the people / asks in the chat / about one of / the lonely panelists / who looks unlike what they think a woman should / punctuation / as ammunition / !?!?

public mourning / says one of the / lonely people / on the panel / can be a / political act / grieving bodies / on streets / in parks / at gatherings / remembering bodies / not suit-ed / for future success /

YOU ARE ENOUGH

Timothy Day

THERE WAS ONE HEART MONITOR in the hospital that wouldn't stop beeping. It just kept on, steady, even after the heart it was monitoring stopped, even after the nurse unplugged it, even after it was stuffed in the back of an out-of-use supply closet, where it had been for years now, faintly beeping behind the door. People died in the reach of its distant rhythm; babies were born into its muffled constancy.

I sometimes stopped in front of that closet, just to make sure the monitor was still beeping. I'd come to think of it like the beating of the world's subconscious heart. For it to stop would surely be the worst of omens, but there it was, always, promising to outlive us all.

Ms. Nilsout was in the late stages of her illness. I was in charge of checking her vitals, which I did every four hours. They'd put her in the worst room of the poor-and-dying wing, the room for those without visitors, the one with cracks in the walls and quickest access to the morgue.

Her family was in Florida, she kept saying, which is why they hadn't been to see her.

"They're chasing the alligators in Florida," she told me. "We're a family of gator hunters."

"That's pretty cool," I said.

Ms. Nilsout huffed. "It's cool as shit."

The hospital had tried calling her brother several times, but he just hung up the phone when he heard who it was. There was no one else. If Ms. Nilsout wasn't dead by tomorrow, she'd be rolled out to the street and left there. I wondered, hopefully, if maybe she'd rather be outside anyway, if maybe there would be a pretty sunset just when she was passing. But when you're alone, a pretty sunset is still just a pretty sunset.

Evening came, and Ms. Nilsout still wasn't dead. After checking her vitals I asked my supervisor, Greg, if I could talk to him about her.

"Like, about where to leave her tomorrow?" Greg asked. He wore round glasses over his small, punchy eyes.

"No."

"Because I told you where to leave her, Ethan."

"I know."

"Just on the sidewalk next to the overpass."

"Right."

We stood in the hallway outside her room. The lights were dimmer here than in the rest of the hospital. Across the way were the old supply closet and the stairway to the morgue.

"I was wondering if we could keep her here a little longer," I said.

Greg shook his head. "I don't understand."

"Just until she passes on," I said.

"Her release date is tomorrow."

"But there's nobody to take her."

"Correct," Greg said. "Which is why you're leaving her by the overpass. Did you forget where to leave her?"

"No, I just—"

"I can remind you tomorrow morning."

"That's not the issue."

"All good then." Greg smiled. "Maybe write yourself a note, like *overpass*, with a little drawing of the patient beside it. That helps me sometimes." He patted me on the shoulder and made his way back up the hallway.

Ms. Nilsout felt different, though she shouldn't have; we'd all had to leave patients on the street before, usually beside the overpass. I guess I felt like we had a sort of connection. Most of the people I tended to didn't speak much; they were either too sad or physically unable to. Ms. Nilsout would tell me stories, though, ask about my life, and sometimes she would make a joke about the hospital food and we would share a laugh. I was moved by her persistence in putting pain beneath a pillow. Like, it wasn't that her family didn't care about her, it was that they were gator hunters; it wasn't that she was dying, it was that she'd lived a life full of late nights, and this was just the final morning after; it wasn't that all her friends were dead, it was that they were waiting for her. I understood her need for happily designed fabric covering pits of sad.

After my shift I went down to the morgue to see my friend Tom. I don't know if Tom thought of us as friends, actually, because mostly he didn't look at me or respond when I talked, but I thought he was pretty cool. He had tattoos of beer cans on his palms, and his hair was long like a rock star's.

That night Tom was sitting in the purple armchair beside the cold lockers, his thumb swiping languidly across the screen of his phone. I sat on the floor against the lockers of beef sticks, which is what Tom called the dead bodies.

"I have to leave a patient on the street tomorrow," I said.

Tom stared at his phone, mouth slightly open.

"They don't have anyone to pick them up," I added.

Tom wiped the back of his hand across his nose and sniffed loudly.

"Where do you want to be left," I asked, "when you die?"

"In a bird feeder," Tom said.

I was confused. "How would you fit?"

Tom stared at me blankly. "My ashes, stupid." He slouched farther in the chair and looked back at his phone. "Just grind me up like coffee and put me in there. It'd be, like, a major prank on the birds."

"Oh yeah, duh." I blushed. "That'd be hilarious."

"Fuckin' A," Tom said.

I lived alone. It had been like that for a while. I'd gotten used to it, I guess, though when you get used to something sad it is still sad, just in a way you don't think about as much. In the days of Darren and Alicia, before they decided that they just wanted to be with each other, I would come home to love, and that love would take up all the space inside me as I moved about the apartment. Now I come home and I go along with my aloneness, but still that space wonders: what is going to fill me? It always seems to expect something, even after all this time.

That night I made pasta and ate looking out the window, watching the mother and daughter who played together in the street below my apartment. The daughter had a disfigurement that rendered her features blurry, like someone being interviewed on the news who wants to remain anonymous. The blocky pixels shifted and crackled on her face as she ran around and jumped rope. They often played late at night like this, and I wondered if the mother or daughter was ashamed of the blur, if they both were. I wanted to tell them not to be, but who was I to say that? Shame had keys to all my locks.

In bed, I lay awake and thought about Ms. Nilsout, coughing to herself in that old room at the end of the hospital's poor-and-dying wing. There are stretches of life I imagine to be far crueler than death; the only reason we stay in them is the chance of their end. If only we knew death past the beginning. But I suppose that could be said about most things.

I got to the hospital early the next morning and checked on Ms. Nilsout. Greg was in the room already, looking over a form.

"Just need to check a few more boxes here," he said. "You understand that you do not possess the funds to remain at the Eternal Love Hospital until your imminent death?"

"I understand," Ms. Nilsout said. She looked incredibly frail, having passed into that phase of sickness where one resembles a skeleton more than a living person.

Greg checked a box. "You understand that you have no family willing to let you die in their home or pay for you to remain at the Eternal Love Hospital until the time of your aforementioned imminent death?"

"I understand," Ms. Nilsout said.

"Very good." Greg scribbled something and nodded at me. "She's all yours." He made his way out, stopping at the door and looking back at Ms. Nilsout. "When you get to the other side, say hi to John Lennon for me. I lost my virginity to 'Imagine.'" He stood there grinning for what seemed a long time, then left.

I sat beside Ms. Nilsout and checked her vitals, though it didn't really matter at that point. "I'm going to miss you," I said.

"Yes, yes." Ms. Nilsout nodded. "Let's get on with it."

I wheeled Ms. Nilsout out of the hospital. The sun was still rising outside, and the sky was like grainy orange juice. Tom was taking a smoke break, and I stopped to say hello.

"This the dying lady?" Tom nodded at Ms. Nilsout.

"It is," Ms. Nilsout said.

"I have to take her to the overpass," I said.

Tom flicked his cigarette on the sidewalk. "I'll come," he said. "I need to move around a little."

So the three of us made our way off hospital grounds and down the side of the highway. I wheeled Ms. Nilsout's stretcher as smoothly as I could, but it still bumped around a good bit on the gravelly pavement. Tom shouted over the roar of passing cars, telling us about all the cocaine he'd done last night.

"At one point I was like, fuck! I could fucking fly right now if I wanted to!" he said. "But then I just cleaned my fucking bathroom."

I thought Tom was pretty cute when he got excited like this. Ms. Nilsout had her eyes closed, but she was smiling. I think she was enjoying Tom's story. We approached the overpass, and I weaved Ms. Nilsout around a clutter of abandoned shopping carts.

"I always loved the word *celestial*," Ms. Nilsout said, voice skidding as she rode across the uneven ground. "I suppose dying out here will be kind of celestial in its way."

"I could see that," I said. And I could, maybe. It seemed better to try, anyway.

There was a little chalk outline indicating where to leave patients like Ms. Nilsout, and I steered the stretcher inside of it. Below us, the cars on the freeway were already in gridlock. Their windows glinted angrily in the morning sun. I took a deep breath. I didn't know what to say. Tom leaned against the railing and lit a cigarette.

"So this is it, huh?" Ms. Nilsout said.

"I guess so," I said. "I'm sorry I can't do more, Ms. Nilsout. I—"

"Quiet." Ms. Nilsout patted my wrist. "I'm trying to die." She squeezed her eyes closed and clenched her fists. I joined Tom at the side of the overpass, and we watched Ms. Nilsout willing death to come. Car horns blared from below.

"Let's go." Tom sniffed. "Smells like piss."

"Just give me a second." I went back to Ms. Nilsout, thinking it might be nice for her if I held her hand for a moment. When I did, though, her palm was cold and limp. Her face had gone slack, paler than pale, and when I checked her pulse I felt nothing.

"She's gone," I called to Tom.

"Nice of her to wait until we got all the way out here," Tom huffed. "Might as well drag her ass back."

So I wheeled Ms. Nilsout's body back to the hospital while Tom talked about necrophilia. Apparently he suspected that his cousin Jim was into it. When we got to the hospital, I asked Tom if he would maybe want to have a drink that night. He seemed to be talking to me more than usual.

"Nah," Tom said. "No offense, dude, but you're kind of weird." He took Ms. Nilsout's stretcher from me and headed down to the morgue.

Probably it had just been the cocaine.

I went to the out-of-use supply closet and leaned my head against the door. The heart monitor inside was still beeping away. I imagined Ms. Nilsout becoming a part of it, her heartbeat leaving this world and entering the collective pulse of the monitor. It was a nice thought.

When Darren and Alicia told me they were leaving, I asked them why, as if I didn't know. They were leaving because they loved each other more than they loved me. When they traded glances, there was a new language present in the air between them, one that didn't include me. When they spoke, it was for my benefit, because they both had the words in their heads already.

I said maybe it would come, a love for me that was equal to their love for each other. Maybe it was close behind. They shook their heads, and I screamed into a pillow.

I was nearing the end of my shift when Greg told me there was a new patient in the poor-and-dying wing.

"Hit by a car on her way home from work," he said. "Her daughter's here—really weird kid. All blurry in the face."

"Oh," I said. "I think I know them."

"That right?"

"Well, not exactly," I said. "We're neighbors, I think."

"OK, Ethan, OK!" Greg threw his hands up. "I don't need your whole life story."

I hurried to the woman's room. She was in pretty bad shape, with a broken collarbone and lots of bruises around her ribs. Her daughter sat beside the bed, blurry chin resting on her fist.

"My name's Ethan," I said. "I'm just here to make sure you're doing OK."

"I got hit by a car," the woman said.

"Right," I said, reading her heart monitor. "That was a stupid question, sorry."

"You are enough," said the daughter.

I paused and looked at where her eyes seemed to be. "What?"

She pointed behind me, and I looked over my shoulder. There was a poster of a mountain on the wall, the frame moldy and cracked. I'd seen it a million times but never really looked at it. *You Are Enough* was printed beneath the mountain, which I thought was silly because how could any of us live up to a mountain?

"I don't get it," said the daughter. Her voice sounded like it was coming from underwater.

"I guess it's, like, telling you that you don't need to be anything more than you are to be worthy of love," I said. "You are enough."

The girl's blurry head dipped, and she knocked her dangling shoes together. "Do you believe that?"

"I do," I said. And at that moment, I did. ✧

CARE

Ciona Rouse

He took his body very seriously,
always ran and had pride
in everything he did.
– Ahmaud Arbery's father to ABC News

Today I braided my hair.
Massaged the pads
of my fingers with each slide
down these textured strands.

Today I also took a bath
of bubbles and Epsom salts,
lit candles that created a wild glow
on my skin each time I lifted my leg
and watched the bubbles jazz
their way back to the water.

Today I listened
to Billie Holiday ask a willow tree
to weep on her behalf
and wished nature worked that way,
wished a gardenia could cover
some of my mistakes.

Also today I drank a cup of tea—earl grey.
I read Wanda Coleman poetry,
counted how many
bottles of water I consumed.
I napped.
I ran a few miles
in bright clothes.

I have cried for trees before,
but I never thought to ask one
to drop its leaves for me.

Today I stopped by the sugar maple
before untying my running shoes.
I know you don't have weeping in your name, I said,
but perhaps you might at least tremble.

I sat on one of its roots today.
I repeated names many of us now know to say,
and we both shook—the maple and me.
I pulled loudly on oxygen.
She let me sit there. Breathing.

COUNTRY
OF THE BLIND

Brittany Hailer

WHEN MY FATHER WAS FIVE, he turned to his mother and asked, "Who just turned off all the lights?"

He remembers the bleached sidewalk and the summer breeze and then he remembers nothingness. He'd gone blind just like that, in an instant and with no warning. After an emergency surgery, he was hospitalized for a month. My father regained his vision, but his eyes rolled around in his head for the next year. When someone talked to him, his baby-blues went off in different directions, trying to find the voice. He had to wear inch-thick bifocals that embarrassed him.

When he was eleven, my father was molested by a priest, which resulted in years of addiction and psychological terror.

I grew up Catholic. My father and mother took me to church every Sunday before they got divorced, before Dad slipped into drink and psychosis. I went to CCD classes. I received my first communion. I confessed to a priest in a pine box. I prayed to porcelain Mother Mary statues. My grandmother hosted priests and nuns, offering them cold Coca-Colas and sandwiches.

Imagine my father in the wooden pew, in a starched shirt, avoiding eye contact with the priest and clergymen. Imagine his neck red against the stiff collar my mother had ironed, never knowing his past.

At night, when he raged and smashed dinner plates or punched drywall, my mother would come into my room and stroke my brow. She'd sing "Amazing Grace" until I fell asleep.

I once was lost, but now am found. Was blind, but now I see.

In my mid-twenties, my father was on the brink of homelessness. His addiction had plateaued for years, but after he lost his job, it escalated into week-long binges. During that time, I had a recurring dream where I taught a blind man to swim.

I carried him on my back in a giant indoor pool made of marble and gold. The man was frail, bird-boned, paper-skinned, his eyes the milky-blue of prophets. His thin arms hung around my neck as we submerged. Later, I cradled him. Chest up, he rested his head back into the water and smiled. I told him to breathe in, and hold. I pulled his face below the surface.

His eyes opened, milk-blue under blue.

Blind sight: In a study where researchers explored the existence of a sixth sense, participants who were blind sat in front of television screens that flashed the faces of different people. When asked what expressions the faces were making, the participants didn't know. However, as the photos changed on the screen, their faces mimicked the facial expressions on the monitors.

Our eyes can sense expression and feeling and pain without a conscious understanding.

The organ that is the eye is the physical embodiment of empathy.

My grandmother told my father that he was some kind of psychic. He didn't get it from her, but from his dad, Red Dog. He was a firefighter with red hair who bruised his children. But he softened in old age and called me his Mona Lisa. Red saw things. Knew things. Dreamed things. Dad calls it Red Intuition. Dad says he wishes every day that his father had known about the priest.

My father told me for years that he'd wind up either in a mental institution or dead by his own hand. Neither of those things ended up being true.

I wonder whether his boy-body tried to go blind before the thing that happened to him.

My dad remembers the nurse unwrapping the bandages from his eyes, layer by layer. The first thing he saw was his father. Red sat in a chair by the bed in his Arlington County firefighter uniform.

"Damn, boy, can you see me?" his father said.

Our eyes are connected to our amygdala, where emotions are processed and stored in our brains. The amygdala is one of the first parts we form. It's old. It records, sometimes remembering trauma that happened before we formed language. We saw something as a child we don't have words for. But our body hasn't forgotten.

I didn't tell my father about my own sexual assault until my book was accepted for publication. The book was about his assault and subsequent addiction and how, later, he got sober and survived. I called him to tell him the truth, a secret I had kept hidden for more than a decade.

When I told him he fell silent, the phone a valley between us.

He gasped for air and said, "I knew. I knew. I always knew. I had dreams for years. I knew."

"I didn't think you guys knew what was going on. It always happened at night. You were asleep," my mother said.

My therapist had been working me back through my memories, trying to find the first, searching for what made me so afraid of sleep. My mother tells me I was born into chaos. My father disappeared for the first week of my life, only to reappear as a broken window. My mom slept on the couch as he climbed in. He grinned, cocksure, and opened the fridge like he didn't have an infant daughter upstairs whom he hadn't yet met. Mom, furious, threw a glass of water on him.

He grabbed a knife.

He chased her up the stairs to my crib. She ran with me wrapped in her arms, out of the house, into a car. She sped her way to my grandmother. We lived with Nana for several months.

Do I have this memory? Did my body collect these nights in my veins and cells and bury them into the folds of where consciousness is first developed?

My mother tells me that I slept with my eyes open as a toddler. She'd wake and find me, eyelids peeled back, irises flickering back and forth, rotating, floating in circles. Sometimes I'd mouth words to the darkness. She and my grandmother would joke that I was possessed.

When I grew and learned to walk, I started waking up and climbing into her bed.

"My god. You've been doing this your whole life," she said.

Nearly thirty years later, my therapist suggested that I start eye movement desensitization and reprocessing (EMDR) treatment to reprocess my sexual assault. It's a psychotherapy designed to alleviate stress related to traumatic memories.

During an EMDR session, a therapist asks me to focus on a negative thought, memory, or image. In my hands, two tappers buzz back and forth. This is called bilateral stimulation. While the rhythm alternates from hand to hand, I am asked to let my mind wander. When the memories bubble forth, I'm asked, "What do you notice?"

Patients are encouraged to close their eyes during EMDR, but I am too afraid. During a session, I can see the garage where I was taken and assaulted, but my eyes are open, wide open.

Over time, the distress over particular thoughts, images, or memories starts to reprocess. The fear response weakens and becomes neutral.

I remember the garage. I can still see it, but my chest no longer seizes and the room doesn't bottom out. My triggers still exist, but they are less lethal.

When I think about this treatment, the eyes, the tapping, I wonder, what did I *see* in the ceiling as a child?

✧

My father's condition as a child was nystagmus, "dancing eyes." Doctors haven't pinpointed the cause of the condition, but they know it is linked to the brain. Many are born with it, but some develop symptoms later in life. It's rarely a cause for surgical intervention, and my father wishes his parents were still alive so he could ask them about what happened. Nystagmus is often genetic but can also be a result of trauma.

Nystagmus can occur in adults with alcoholism and drug addiction. In my memoir and in journals from when I was a child, I would write that my father's eyes danced around in his head.

✧

"The Country of the Blind" is a short story by H. G. Wells. It was first published in 1904.

A mountaineer named Nunez falls down the far side of an unconquered mountain, where he finds an isolated community. The inhabitants of the valley have been blind for generations after a disease struck early settlers. The town is fully adapted to life without sight.

Nunez discovers this and recites to himself, "In the Country of the Blind, the One-eyed Man is King."

But Nunez is labeled a madman because of his obsession with this thing called "sight." The village doctor examines Nunez and finds a troublesome organ causing Nunez's sickness.

The village doctor tells the elders:

"Those queer things that are called the eyes, and which exist to make an agreeable depression in the face, are diseased, in the case of Nunez, in such a way as to affect his brain. They are greatly distended, he has eyelashes, and his eyelids move, and consequently his brain is in a state of constant irritation and distraction . . . And I think I may say with reasonable certainty that, in order to cure him complete, all that we need to do is a simple and easy surgical operation—namely, to remove these irritant bodies."

"And then he will be sane?"

"Then he will be perfectly sane, and a quite admirable citizen."

I could not write about my parents for years. One night, when I started writing the book that would attempt to tell our story— the abuse, the priest, the drinking, the forgiveness—I lost my vision. Literally. I could not see the screen or the words. I turned my head up toward the ceiling, my eyes twitching back and forth. It happened over and over.

I wrote our story blind. It was the only way my body knew how. Perhaps it couldn't remember with my eyes open. Perhaps the body can see only so much at once, and to dive into the valley, into the depths of the dark thing that made me, a second sight was required. Perhaps the eyes are a distraction. Perhaps the quitting eyes are an inheritance.

My fingers tapped across the keyboard and my sight snapped shut, like someone had just turned off all the lights. ✧

SPLITTING
THE CRACKS

Claire Denson

I want to call its flaked limbs dead—
the tree outside that knocks
against the fogged glass. Knuckles
drier than bone, easier to snap.

I want to snap your bones
while we lie in bed, make two
out of one, so you can bend
in new ways. I want to give you

more bones, unmerge the merged,
a chance to begin again. We can
make flour out of anything
if we grind it down. Bone flour,

bark flour. The reaching tree
outside survives tall, protesting
its barrenness. In this bed I'm bare,
stripped down, wintered raw,

my touch cold as the pane
against the branch's caress.
You hold out my hand, expose
each finger, slip yours through

my cracks, and when I think to ask
if the morning makes your bones heavy,
makes them creak like dry wood
under work boots, you tell me it's time

for breakfast, let's make pancakes, let's
stay in. I roll back my palm, say I'll make
the batter. I taste your teeth
from your kiss, your bones

in my mouth. Pancake made of bone. Pancake
tasting like kisses. Eating pancakes of you, with
you, toothless. The wind shoves the hard
crown of the tree and it pounds down

this time, no longer asking
but begging: Let me in. I turn my back
but you, you reach
over me, you crack the pane.

WEDDING VOWS
FIRST DRAFT

Claire Denson

I sent my wisdom teeth in the mail
labeled *from the tooth fairy*
but my friends received empty envelopes
with holes punched through. I have since learned

it is illegal to mail body tissue
through USPS. I think about those teeth,
the one shaped like a dancer
with its molar roots tilted sideways

like little ballet legs, the one that crumbled
into three, each part bloody
and rotten. Who holds them tonight?
Lying in the surgeon's chair

I sobbed over "Imagine" playing
through the speakers. *It's a lie*,
I said. I understand that I was high
but I still can't shake the feeling

of my pain ignored. When the surgeon
said *it's over* I asked for my teeth back
and he gawked at me like I was the first
to request a return. Has he previously

thrown them all out in some waste bin
labeled *toxic*? I saved one tooth for years
until parting with it today as a gift
to the one I love. I like that he holds

what could be my remains. My last
wisdom tooth, the nicest one, its softness
somewhere between pearl and diamond,
and more rare than both. I wrapped it

in a plastic tooth-shaped tooth-coffin
that I've saved with the treasure-spirit
of an old woman who stows away
a family heirloom for that wistful

one day. Is romance to be found
in dentistry? Is love a form of letting
go? *All I know is myself*, I think
as I take his hand.

DUTY

Jax Connelly

MY COFFEE IS BURNT AND TOO HOT to drink but I take a sip anyway, because it's a matter of minutes before it cools to the temperature of a cashed bowl deserted on a windowsill. It's a matter of hours before my Bluetooth headphones start interrupting my womp-womp indie folk to beep-boop about how I've drained the battery. The tops of my hands are so dry they're cracking, on the verge of splitting open. Everything is always on the verge of something else.

A stocky man with a salt-and-pepper beard walks in with what looks like a middle schooler's backpack slung over one shoulder. He surveys the room and issues a cheerful "Good morning!" The girl with the pink highlights mumbles a reply. A few people shift in their chairs, avoiding eye contact, while I glare kidney stones from the corner. Is salt-and-pepper hair the only thing that reminds me of my dad? He went half-gray before his thirtieth birthday. When I forget to shave my head every two weeks, I remember I'm my father's daughter.

This is the second day of jury duty. I'm Juror 861. All of us are on edge; all of us are in between. Yesterday, Jurors 86 and 859 were called in the last group. For nine hours, I didn't leave my plastic seat except to go to the bathroom.

Actually, folk music reminds me of my dad, too. This music in my headphones—the only soundtrack that's appropriate for drab little rooms lined with ransacked vending machines, stripped bare by fluorescent lights. It's the updated version of what he used to play on his guitar, downstairs in his den while I was falling asleep, gentle acoustics floating up through the heat vents like stray feathers from my pillow: Harry Chapin; Simon & Garfunkel; Peter, Paul and Mary; John Denver; Gordon Lightfoot. All my favorite songs fall into this genre; all declare something simple and gutting like "Scott & Zelda" by Tiny Victories: *That's how it goes—I guess it's all right. You have something, then you lose it for the rest of your life.*

My sister and I have a running joke called Potato Dad. It's not clever or creative—it's exactly how it sounds. It's comparing our dad to a potato, because potatoes don't do much. They just sit there like sad little lumps, growing soft and wrinkly.

I read a whole book yesterday, sitting here in this room. I was so bored it made me angry—the fury of inertia, blanks expecting to be filled. I scribbled hateful notes all over the pages. I left my headphones on even when they started beep-booping, even when they turned themselves off. I refused to make eye contact with anyone, even when I could tell they were craving it.

"Not my circus. Not my monkeys." That's what my mom would say. I haven't spoken to her in years. I understand why I can't call her—there are too many wounds that can't remember how to be regular skin. But I don't understand why I can't call my dad. There are no wounds. Or maybe that's the wound: that hollow place, that lack.

The old man with the thick wooden cane is back today. He limps over to the table next to mine and sets his Smithsonian grocery bag gently on the tile floor. He drapes his highlighter-yellow jacket over the back of a chair, then pulls it out carefully as if he's determined to not wake a baby, moving his arms the way you move them when you're carrying a very hot, very full cup of coffee down the hall.

I can see him, my dad, bright-eyed, explaining the solution to this very hot, very full cup of coffee scenario. "I have a special trick for that. Do you want to know the special trick?"

When you're growing up, Potato Dad leaves the feelings and the fighting and the discipline to your mom. Potato Dad stays out of the way. He works a lot because your mom doesn't and because it's his duty to provide. He comes home late and locks himself in his den, where he plays his guitar or reads biographies of presidents and war heroes or flies simulated airplanes on his computer. Potato Dad is like the bystander effect: he's not contributing to the crime, but he's not doing anything to stop it, either.

A black athletic shirt stretches over the old man's potbelly, tucked snug into his khaki pants. He's wearing an expensive watch. He unscrews a disposable plastic water bottle, the kind that always ends up in the gutter or a filthy stream or teetering on top of an overstuffed garbage can on a busy street corner downtown. He takes a grateful gulp and opens a library book, all of it crinkling like my great-grandmother's furniture.

Actually, mustaches remind me of my dad, too. I've never seen him without one. Generally I feel hard toward men, closed off and skeptical, but a mustache makes me soft. A mustache on an old man makes me want to weep and look away and pretend there is no such thing as old men with mustaches or fathers with daughters or daughters who renounce their fathers or fathers who hardly notice when it happens.

Everything is always on the verge of something else. Before he was Potato Dad, my dad was a romantic, a dreamer, a creative. He taught himself guitar. He won a song-writing competition. He double-majored in Spanish and German at Georgetown and then he went to business school and then he sold truck parts for the rest of his life.

You Won't, "Realize": *Wasn't I gonna be digging up hidden treasure, instead of burying change in the mud?*

Yesterday, after checking in, I rode the elevator with the old man. "First time?" he asked, smiling mildly, like we were reading a script. "What gave it away?" I played along, gesturing around at my bulky headphones and my shaved head and my combat boots. He chuckled like I'd given him a delightful little gift, a stocking stuffer or one of those Precious Moments statuettes.

My dad was summoned for jury duty when I was a kid. His boss told him to get out of it no matter what he had to do, and it would have been easy—the plaintiff or the defendant was a former client of my dad's; they had worked together in some capacity. But the judge asked if that would affect my dad's ability to be objective in the case, and my dad shrugged and told the truth: "No."

Later, when the old man caught my eye and waved at me from across the room, I pretended not to see. When they dismissed us for lunch and he stopped in front of my table, I pretended to be immersed in something on my laptop. When they sent us home for the day, when he waited and waited until I gathered my belongings and I had no choice but to remove my dead headphones, I swallowed back the sadness trying to inch its way up through my mouth, like a glass stem lodged in my throat.

My dad didn't go in too hard for emotional expression, but he cried every year on Christmas Eve when we watched *It's a Wonderful Life* and Harry Bailey gives the toast at the end: "To my big brother, George—the richest man in town!" He cried when he got the call that his own dad was dying of lung cancer, and he cried when I sealed myself in the bathroom after the first time I tried to kill myself. He unlocked the sliding door with the butt of a nail clipper and collapsed on the tile floor gulping down loud, wet sobs, and I stepped over him carefully and hid in my closet instead.

"How was it? How was your first day?" the old man asked me, with a smile. "Boring," I replied, without one. He stepped into the elevator and held the door for me. I replaced my headphones and took the stairs.

Typhoon, "Artificial Light": *I was told that I'd grow up to be myself. I thought I would get bigger, too.*

When you think about Potato Dad, you mostly think about absence, which isn't necessarily fair. He can't cook, but he can make you "eggie toastie": scrambled eggs, white toast with butter on the side. He can show you how to make mac and cheese from a box: After you drain the noodles, leave them in the colander in the sink and put the pot back on the stove. Turn the heat as low as it can go and drop in the butter. When it starts to melt, add the powdered cheese and a little bit of milk. Mix it up nice and smooth before you reunite it with the noodles—it'll be cheesier, he swears. Potato Dad is there at all the important events: your softball games, your piano recitals, your high-school graduation. He smiles for the camera, but only with his mouth.

The song that won the competition is "The Master," which requires a lot of intricate fingerpicking and recounts a tale of love lost to ambition. But my favorite of my dad's originals is

"Doc's Lament." It's about an old man who owns a coffee shop and tries to engage his younger patrons in conversation, but pretty much no one is interested. I click on my dad's Spotify page and stare at the ">1,000 monthly listeners." I play this song over and over, and I think about how I see the old man from jury duty everywhere, how I can't look him in the eye. He's been emptied out by the years; he's a fallen pine that made a racket none of us heard. He's retired and alone and no one asks him what he thinks anymore and now he's just waiting to die.

I can see him, my dad, dignified, voted foreman of his jury. He's safe from his boss for weeks, relaying stories from the case every night at the dinner table, face lighting up like he's performing an encore.

Frightened Rabbit, "Poke": *You should look through some old photos—I adored you in every one of those.*

I cringe to confess it, but the glass in my throat that grieves for the elderly is heterosexist. Old women, I assume, have always known no one cares what they think. Old women are like my mom: hard and mean and far more resilient than their aging husbands could ever hope to be. What kind of duty do daughters owe their mothers, their fathers? My parents are old and getting older. "Not my circus. Not my monkeys."

I have failed, again and again, at being the correct kind of mother's daughter. That's why I haven't talked to my dad in years, either—he couldn't stand for it. Or he wouldn't. Or what's the difference? I was expecting the call because I had just had my first essay published—finally, something to push our relationship into greater depths. Look, Dad, we are both artists. But he talked at me as if I were still the teenager who slammed their door so many times my mom took it off its hinges, as if I were still ruled by my hysterical amygdala. Everything is always on the verge of something else, but that doesn't mean it always gets there.

It's strange to be stuck in this room for so long with people I'll never see again, all of us having nothing to do with one another. Like this guy in the blue polo shirt, sitting directly across from me—he doesn't appear to be doing anything besides staring at the wall. He's not even scrolling through his phone or sipping from his Nalgene. He's just sitting there like he's resigned himself to exactly how everyone's life turns out: all these arbitrary collisions. I try to memorize his face, but I know I wouldn't recognize him on the street.

Were there real moments, between the two of us? There must have been. I suppose it matters that he taught me how to drive before I was old enough, in his station wagon in the empty parking lot next to the Sears, and how to play both parts of "Heart and Soul" on the piano at the same time, and that an apple is nature's toothbrush. I must have made him laugh, once or twice. He must have shared some fatherly wisdom more helpful than "Red sky at night, sailor's delight; red sky in morning, sailors take warning" and "She's the only mother you've got." There may have been something true, some deeper access point, unlocked in old board games such as Stratego, in how delighted he was that time I chased one of his top dogs around the field with a mere scout and he found out I'd been bluffing. "That's exactly how you have to play this game," he kept saying, chuckling and grinning, over the moon, perhaps the proudest I ever saw him.

When things are looking bleak, Potato Dad says something like, "You just gotta have faith." During the whole four years you're in college, he calls just once to ask, earnestly, "So, how's the bulimia?" He pronounces it bew-LEEM-ee-uh. When he's nearing retirement, he sends group emails containing photos of the mechanic's workshop he organized: everything in its right place. Potato Dad rarely gets angry or particularly joyful. Sometimes he seems sad, but he can't put his finger on it, so neither can you. Mostly he sits and stares. Mostly he's unbothered.

I didn't realize, when I started writing it, that this was an essay about my dad. Everything is always on the verge of something else. On the phone that night, grown a full decade out of teenage tantrums, I became hysterical. I hurled my Android across the room, the screen cracked, I never spoke to him again, and I'm still not sure what, exactly, it is we've both lost.

Jess Williamson, "Snake Song": *Bind your mother's name to your two wrists, and feel your father's strength in your lover's kiss.*

What kind of duty does a father owe his daughter? My mother's name is old-world Italian, like all my features, but it's been years since I mistook my father for strong. I don't believe in men protecting their families. I don't believe in gender roles or "blood is thicker than water," so I guess what that leaves is: not much.

My number is never called. Neither is the old man's. When the announcement comes over the loudspeaker that we are all permanently dismissed, everyone files out of the room but the two of us. "Are you a writer for a living?" he asks me, sheepishly, like he's expecting me to give him the finger. I almost choke on the glass and it's not even there, so I tell him I am. I tell him I've been working for an insurance magazine for six years, but I'm about to return to school to get a degree in creative writing. He tells me he worked for an insurance company his whole life. He tells me his daughter went to school in Utah. "She was an athlete," he explains, standing up a little straighter. "No debt."

Maybe my dad should have been a diplomat or a history professor or a writer of biographies. Maybe my dad should have remained a bachelor, giving cheap guitar lessons and eating cold pizza for breakfast. Maybe I should never have been born. Maybe this skinny life is as happy as my dad could hope to get, but maybe some other life would have suited him better. Maybe my dad is a lonely soul. Maybe loneliness feels better on some of us than others. Maybe happiness is not the pinnacle we all believe it to be.

I wonder whether the old man would have thought about his daughter today if he hadn't run into me. It's not easy to bear the way your parents see you, but I could never bear the weight of a child, the expectations folding in on themselves, the inevitable betrayal.

Jim Croce, "Operator": *Let's forget about this call. There's no one there I really wanted to talk to.*

In the foyer, they call the old man's number for processing: 841. They call my number directly after, which feels like a strange coincidence. We will be paid twelve dollars for each day of our service: a total of twenty-four. "Don't spend it all in one place," the voice on the loudspeaker jokes—a regular Potato Dad. Everyone laughs gratefully. It's the middle of the day, so there is no traffic on the drive home.

I wonder whether my dad ever thinks about me. I wonder whether he talks about me to strangers he meets at jury duty, at church, in line at the grocery store. Most people assume I don't have a relationship with my parents because I'm queer, and every time I don't correct them, every time I call myself an orphan and wax poetic about chosen family, I feel ashamed and unmoored, like I've committed a crime.

The special trick for the very hot, very full cup of coffee is this: Look up, away from what you're holding, and walk normally. Move forward as if you're not holding anything at all. ✧

THE CURRENCY OF SECRETS

Ruyi Wen

WHEN WE FIRST DISCOVER THEM, we cup them in our palms like gleaming cowrie shells. Each one is magical and precious, though we do not yet know why. On the playground, we tilt them gently into each other's ears, gifts given freely without guile or guilt.

At sleepovers, we hide under the covers and pull them from their hiding places, turning them over and over, studying every detail by flashlight. We slowly sound out words like *shekel* and *tongbei* and *daric*—hard consonants for hard currency—and erupt in giggles when our stubby tongues twist over *numismatics*.

The grown-ups look at us huddling in the corner, a tangle of long hair and longer legs. *How cute*, they say, *the girls are sharing secrets.* Our eyes roll and thumbs scroll. Sharing is for communists. We learn how to mine our midnight thoughts for raw ore, how to stamp and engrave the metal into beautiful designs with sharp reliefs. We hide the coins deep in our pockets, rubbing them between our fingers until their rims are worn smooth, their luster a tarnished amber. When the opportunity strikes, we pull them out to pay for memberships in exclusive sisterhoods. We trade, sell, and exchange them for what they're worth. Loyalties. Allegiances. A place a little closer to the center of the circle.

We rule by fiat, building an empire on our currency of secrets. Envious barbarian whispers dart among slamming locker doors, but we know they all just want to be one of us. We cross our arms and look down our patrician noses at them, asking: *Do you support free trade? How will you contribute to the economy? Do you swear to support and defend our intricate monetary system, for richer or poorer, so help you God?* Fortune favors the bold. The reserved ones never make it in.

The boys, sensing there is money to be made, whisper sweet nothings of love me tender in our ears. They claim to be chief economists, artisan engravers, expert notaphilists, whatever they think we might need. They show us coin designs we have never seen and try to talk us into their unorthodox, self-serving monetary theories. *I will appreciate your currency tenfold*, they swear. We scrutinize the promises and vote on them in committee. *Yes. No. Maybe.*

As our empire expands, the whispers grow louder and louder until they are a persistent, frenzied buzzing. The sounds stop abruptly when we approach, like the chirping of paranoid crickets.

Until one day, in the silence, a heretic laughs in disbelief, and suddenly everyone follows.

In an instant, we discover our economy runs on a trust that has been broken. Our innermost desires and fears have turned into crumpled old bills, common and worthless, stuffed in the smirking mouths of strangers like so much paper money to be burned.

The coins have been debased, the wealth destroyed, the secrets spent. But not for nothing. Now we know who can be trusted, and who has betrayed us. If there is a next time, we will build our walls of foreign exchange controls ten feet higher.

The economy teetering on the edge of depression, we slip into the darkness of gym bleachers, side alleys, websites browsed on incognito mode by men with glinting eyes and heavy breaths, and print more money using the ink of night. ✧

I STAR IT OUT

Erika Walsh

My mother had a tiger's eye she kept tied at her waist. It's protective, she said.
When she cried no one could find her. This was on purpose and also a spell.

There was a witch in our house who was also a ghost. The witch washed her hair often, in the
bathroom sink or kitchen, where we sat cross-legged around a TV. We smelt her splitting hair
made clean. It smelled like pepper flakes   and beetroot.
                    It made our bodies move   like sand.

The witch's spell was unique   it was transformation's opposite

     it created repetition   and tied bodies to a place.

The witch hated my father. He swept dead grass from the floor. Each morning he would
say that's it, oh my god, and I'm moving.

When he tried to leave, a cigarette placed itself in his mouth.

The smoke would bring him to sleep   the witch would comb out his hair.

When he tried to leave, an animal would choose him for a home.

He put out wet food for the deer, and red squirrels. He put out wet food for the birds.

The witch liked my mother. She laughed when she would cook the same dish

as her own   :   white fish over spinach   wilted   garlicked in our mouths

Her laugh sounded like metal. It brought everything close.

Once the witch placed a single yellow thumb inside my mouth.

I was seven, and pretended to be very cool about it.

Later I had nightmares. I wrote them down with wonder

like dark borrowed stories that did not happen to me.

Her thumb in my mouth, I wanted to gag.

She made me taste the white wax she found underneath my tongue.
When held, the wax went cold. It became like a dead thing.
Like oil on a moth's wing you are not supposed to touch.

On waxless nights   sometimes   I would design my own half-spells :

A peeled grape floating   in a vat of golden oil   A machine dreamt out of cardboard
and red marker in a red hand   I was so afraid of prayer   I had to do it every night

God bless mommy and daddy and chrissy and blake   jewels and gemma and star
all our goldfish   all the grass that keeps dying please bless it   please bless judy in her sick
bed please bless   me I would say   at the end   in a small voice

As I got older lovers came over, and friends.
I used to think if I slept next to someone nothing bad could happen.

I said this to an ex who was also a friend. Her hair reaching like arms
to my headboard. That night she said of course   I'll sleep over
        That night the witch tapped   on my spine.

My mouth thickened with milk   I was too unsure to kiss

As my last heartbreak heals I do dream of him most nights.
        This makes me frustrated. I really am healing.
    Last night there was a tattoo of a train inside his arm. I know the dream meant comfort.
A reminder for me   :   this has happened before and will happen again.

Once I got so scared I asked an ex to come over and fuck me.

His lack of deep thought counteracted the witch's spells   the spells were blood-red they required
        a person to go inward

I like falling asleep mid-day after a cigarette. I like swimming down to the bottom of a pool.
    I know this is what makes me the most vulnerable to her.

If the witch had an advice column   this is what I would write her :

W. —

Are you going to haunt me until I press a body to me? Sometimes when I am being asked again and again . . . it is like I am waning. Or like gagging on a thumb. I don't mean that as a dig but what am I supposed to do.

When I get too high I press my nose into a pepper shaker. It's supposed to bring you down. Sometimes I lick salt from my hand. Is that bad? I feel silly just throwing it over.

I'm worried my acupuncturist left a needle in my neck. It gets dark at 2 p.m. now. Do you think of your spells or just make them?

When I was young, my parents were both beautiful. You met them. They did headstands and crunches and pull-ups every day.

I wanted beauty too, and so swallowed a button of fruit. I puked until I saw the fruit, blue, wet in my acid. Does this make you sad? Are you thinking of stars.

The last time I slept in the house, I was next to an ex who was also a friend. We did not fuck, and had not yet. We just slept near each other. In the dream I had you pulled me by a black rope to the closet. I was frightened. I am frightened even writing this down, and I'm frightened as I'm reading it over again.

You knew I would be frightened. Why did you show that to me? As a child, and as an adult, I don't like to be shown what I have no control over.

—E.

The word witch feels too strong

I want to star it out.

I wonder if this impulse is internalized misogyny.

When I am in pain I say that I am angry.

I ask you not to talk.

I can't take any more inside me.

    You say you're not attractive when you get like this   [I star it out]

W.—

One last thing—when you're heartbroken, do you write spells in second person?   When I was in eighth grade I traced my crushes' names   over the skin of my leg.   It was always something

short like   nick   dana   joe   it was easy to trace it again and again.

I cast a spell that worked once. I was surprised by its working. Red petals over the screen of my phone, and he came.

I left long red marks over the skin of his back, what is it about witches and long nails, what do you think? Am I making a deal over nothing?

—E.

My mother makes her own toothpaste from oil and from powder.

She texts   :   why do I always have such sensitive emotions?

I want to ask the witch but I don't think that she would know.

I think spells are concerned less with emotion, more with feeling.

E.—

Last night I sent your father one last dream that should fix everything. I meant to show him something red. It turned itself to green. Look—heartbreak is just like any other discomfort. If your chest hurts press a cold pack to it; alternate with heat. I am busy—I don't mean to be this dismissive—if you had a needle still inside your neck I think you'd feel it.

—W.

My last acupuncture session was the first time I didn't cry.

I tried very hard to think   about you kissing someone else.

I'm doing exposure therapy on myself. My insurance gives me lists of dead

or very busy people   when I ask for the name of someone else who can help.

A white light was turning yellow   turning green inside my mouth

You were kissing someone else.

Soon I will dye my hair a deep green for the chakra, and the symbol. That's how the

witch will know I got her message and say thanks.

When I was young I very often chose to leave my dreams. I'd just say a chant or I'd open a door.

I had one that was recurring. I'd be standing on a shore.

Orcas would jump up from the ocean. Dive again and again.

They were beautiful, but as they got closer, I'd leave.

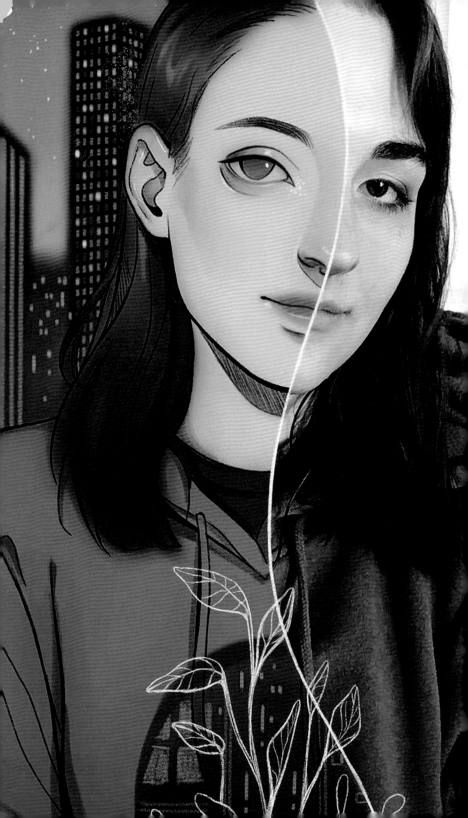

HAYLEE MORICE

Haylee Morice is a freelance artist raised and living in rural Utah. Her illustrations include themes of growth and pain, eerie cityscapes, and everyday beauty. Her style is influenced by artists she admires like James Jean and Heikala, as well as everyday pleasures and places she'd like to visit. While primarily a digital artist, she also enjoys experimenting with traditional mediums, like watercolor, colored pencil, and oil paint. Haylee earned a bachelor's degree in Art & Visual Communications from Utah Valley University in 2017. She now focuses on creating art, growing an audience, and selling her work online and at conventions around the US. More at: hayleemorice.com.

ART

Night Ride . . . . COVER

Dead End Diner 4

Escalator 25

Rooftop 48

Cookies 70

We Hear You 76

Surrender 92

Vending Machines 103

Anywhere 114

Handrail 126

Laundry Day 138

Candy 148

CONTRIBUTORS

DAVID BRUNSON has an MFA in Poetry and Literary Translation from the University of Arkansas. His poems and translations have appeared in or are forthcoming from *Mānoa: A Pacific Journal of International Writing*, *On the Seawall*, *The Bitter Oleander*, *Nashville Review*, *Asymptote*, *Copper Nickel*, *The Literary Review*, *Los Poetas del 5*, and *Temporary Archives: Poems by Women of Latin America*. He is the editor of *Una cicatriz donde se escriben despedidas*, an anthology of Venezuelan migrant poets in Chile, forthcoming from Libros del Amanecer.

EMILIE COLLYER lives in Australia on unceded Wurundjeri land where she writes poetry, plays, and prose. Her work has been published and presented in a broad range of contexts, locally and internationally. She has published one poetry collection, *Your Looking Eyes*, two short fiction collections, and her award-winning plays include *Contest*, *Dream Home*, and *The Good Girl*, which has had multiple international productions. She is a current PhD candidate at RMIT (Naarm/Melbourne), where she is researching feminist creative practice.

JAX CONNELLY (they/she) is an award-winning writer whose creative nonfiction explores the intersections of queer identity, unstable bodies, and mental illness. Their work has received honors including Notables in the Best American Essays 2021 and 2019, Nowhere's Fall 2020 Travel Writing Prize, first place in the 2019 Prairie Schooner Creative Nonfiction Essay Contest, and the 2018 Pinch Literary Award for Creative Nonfiction. Her experimental and hybrid essays have also appeared or are forthcoming in *[PANK]*, *The Rumpus*, *Hunger Mountain*, *Ruminate*, *Pleiades*, and more. Learn more at jaxconnelly.wixsite.com/writer.

STEVEN ESPADA DAWSON is from East Los Angeles and lives in Austin, Texas. He is the son of a Mexican immigrant and is a 2021 Ruth Lilly and Dorothy Sargent Rosenburg Fellow. His recent poems appear in *The Adroit Journal*, *Gulf Coast*, *Kenyon Review Online*, *POETRY*, *Split Lip*, *Waxwing*, and the 2020 *Best New Poets* anthology.

TIMOTHY DAY lives with his plants in Portland, Oregon. He holds an MFA in creative writing from Portland State University, and his fiction has appeared in *The Adroit Journal*, *Barren Magazine*, *Jet Fuel Review*, and elsewhere. You can find links to his work here: neutralspaces.co/timothyday.

CLAIRE DENSON'S poems appear in *Hobart, Massachusetts Review, Sporklet, Salt Hill Journal, the minnesota review, Peach Mag,* and elsewhere. She reads for *The Adroit Journal* and lives in Brooklyn, NY.

BRITTANY HAILER is a journalist and educator based in Pittsburgh, Pennsylvania. She is the director of the Pittsburgh Institute for Nonprofit Journalism. Her memoir and poetry collection *Animal You'll Surely Become* was published by Tolsun Books in 2018. Brittany has taught creative writing classes at the Allegheny County Jail and Sojourner House as part of Chatham's Words Without Walls program and now teaches creative writing and journalism at the University of Pittsburgh. Her work has appeared in *Sierra Club Magazine, Fairy Tale Review, Longform, Hobart, Barrelhouse,* and elsewhere.

ROCHELLE HURT is the author of the poetry collections *The J Girls: A Reality Show* (Indiana University Press, 2022), which won the Blue Light Books Prize from *Indiana Review; In Which I Play the Runaway* (Barrow Street, 2016), which won the Barrow Street Poetry Prize; and *The Rusted City* (White Pine, 2014). Her work has been included in *Poetry* magazine and the *Best New Poets* anthology. She's been awarded prizes and fellowships from *Arts & Letters, Poetry International,* Vermont Studio Center, Jentel, and Yaddo. Hurt lives in Orlando and teaches in the MFA program at the University of Central Florida.

ABBY JOHNSON is a poet and a Hoosier who is proud of the local art scene that fostered her. She received her MFA in Creative Writing through Butler University. During her time there, she served as poetry co-editor for *Booth.* Her micro-chapbook *No Line Except* was published through Ghost City Press in its summer 2019 collection. Her chapbook *Opportunity Cost* will be published through Frontier Poetry in May 2021. She has individual pieces published in *Turnpike Magazine, Josephine Quarterly, The Indianapolis Review,* and most recently the Winter/Spring 2020 issue of *Sycamore Review.*

ALLISON KADE is a Pushcart Prize-nominated fiction writer. Her short stories have appeared in *The Huffington Post* and literary magazines such as *Joyland Magazine, The Massachusetts Review, The Citron Review, Flash Fiction Magazine, Annalemma, Fractured West, After the Pause,* and more. She lives outside of Philadelphia and is currently working on a novel.

TAYLOR KIRBY is a writer from Denver, Colorado, currently living in Austin, Texas. She is the managing editor at *Porter House Review*, and her writing has appeared in *Cream City Review*, *Hobart*, *Longleaf Review*, and elsewhere.

EMILY LAWSON is a graduate of the MFA program in poetry at the University of Virginia, where, as a Poe/Faulkner Fellow, she taught poetry and edited *Meridian*. A graduate of Hampshire College, she is in the doctoral program in philosophy at the University of British Columbia. Her poetry and lyric essays can be found in *Sixth Finch*, *Indiana Review*, *Thrush*, *Waxwing*, *Muzzle*, *DIAGRAM*, and elsewhere. This is her first fiction publication.

SUSAN LERNER received her MFA in Creative Writing from Butler University. She serves as assistant memoir editor for *Split Lip Magazine*, assistant editor for *Brevity*, and reads for *Creative Nonfiction*, *River Teeth*, *TriQuarterly*, *Bellevue Literary Review*, and *Fourth Genre*. Her work has appeared in *The Rumpus*, *The Believer Logger*, *Painted Bride Quarterly*, *Booth*, and elsewhere. Find her on Twitter and Instagram @susanlitelerner and online at susan-lerner.com.

JILLIAN LUFT is a Florida native residing in Brooklyn. Her creative nonfiction has appeared in *Hobart*, *X-R-A-Y*, *JMWW*, *Barren Magazine*, *The Forge Literary Magazine*, and other publications. Currently, she's working on a memoir about caregiving for her terminally ill mother as a child. You can find more of her writing at jillianluft.com.

KATIE MCMORRIS received her MFA from Purdue University, where she received an Academy of American Poets prize. She is currently pursuing her PhD at Oklahoma State University.

COREY MILLER was a finalist for the F(r)iction Flash Fiction Contest ('20) and shortlisted for the Forge Flash Competition ('20). His writing has appeared in *Pithead Chapel*, *Third Point Press*, *Hobart*, *X-R-A-Y*, and elsewhere. He reads for *TriQuarterly*, *Longleaf Review*, *CRAFT*, and *Barren Magazine*. When not working or writing in Cleveland, Corey likes to take the dogs for adventures. Follow him on Twitter @IronBrewer or at coreymillerwrites.com.

JANE MORTON is a poet based in Tuscaloosa, Alabama, where they recently completed their MFA at the University of Alabama. Their poems are published or forthcoming in *Boulevard, Passages North, Poetry Northwest, Fairy Tale Review, The Offing, Muzzle Magazine, Redivider,* and *The Rupture,* among other journals. They have received a Fulbright Fellowship and a Katharine Bakeless Nason scholarship for the Bread Loaf Environmental Writers Conference.

A. PREVETT is the author of the chapbook *Still, No Grace* (Madhouse Press, 2021). Their recent poetry has been featured in such journals as *West Branch, DIAGRAM, Colorado Review, Denver Quarterly,* and others. They are pursuing an MFA in poetry from Georgia State University, where they serve as editor-in-chief of *New South.* You can find more of their work on their website, aprevett.com.

CIONA ROUSE is the author of the chapbook *Vantablack* (Third Man Books, 2017). Her poetry has appeared in *Oxford American, wildness, NPR Music, The Account,* and other publications. She is poetry editor of *Wordpeace.* Along with poet Kendra DeColo, Rouse hosts the literary podcast *Re\VERB* in Nashville, Tennessee.

EVA STERRETT is a freelance animation artist and illustrator based in NYC. You can follow her and her work on social media @evasterrett or sterretteva.myportfolio.com.

ERIKA WALSH is a poet, writer, and cofounding editor of *A Velvet Giant,* a genreless literary journal. Her work has been featured or is forthcoming in *Hobart, Wax Nine Journal, Hotel Amerika, Brooklyn Poets, Visible Poetry Project, Peach Magazine* and elsewhere. An alumna of the artist residency program at Art Farm Nebraska, she works as an editorial assistant and lives in Brooklyn with her pet cat, Willa.

RUYI WEN'S writing has appeared in *Barren Magazine, The Lowestoft Chronicle, McSweeney's Internet Tendency,* and elsewhere. She lives in Texas.